Garridan's Mate

Etherya's Earth, Book 6.5

By

REBECCA HEFNER

Cover Design: Anthony O'Brien, BookCoverDesign.store
Proofreader: Bryony Leah, www.bryonyleah.com

Contents

To my fellow Hearts Unleashed anthology authors. It was an honor to hit the USA Today bestseller list with you!

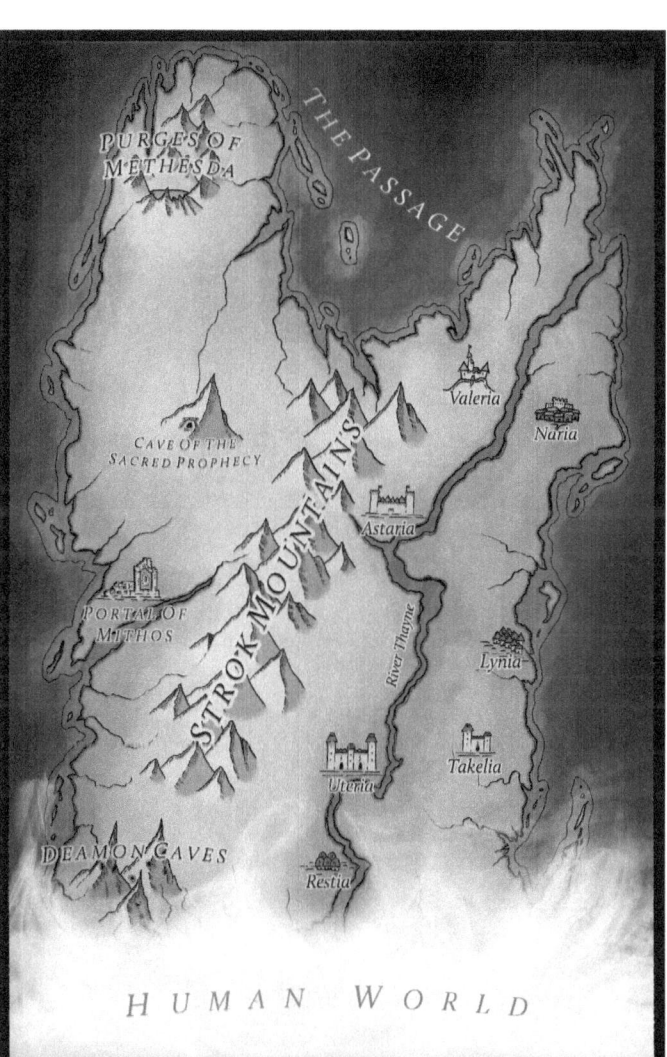

Chapter One

Garridan, son of Astaroth, stood atop the grassy hill observing the field below. Thick arms crossed over his chest as his eyes narrowed. Several soldiers in the vast immortal army were competing to become squadron leaders in the final battle against Bakari. The long-lost Vampyrc royal sibling had a massive army of his own and was intent on defeating them so he could rule in perpetuity. Garridan was determined to prevent that at all costs.

"How's the competition going?" a deep baritone asked.

"Excellent, Commander," Garridan said with a nod. "Radomir and Cian have won the majority of the physical contests as expected, with Siora close behind. The three of them excelled at the obstacle courses, the written leadership exam, and the hand-to-hand fights, although

Cian did get a nasty black eye that took two hours to heal even with his self-healing abilities."

"You can call me Latimus, you know?" the commander said, arching a brow under his black hair, slicked back into a tiny tail secured by a leather strap. "We've fought together since the Awakening. Although we're both technically aristocrats, you know I hate the formal shit."

Garridan smiled into his friend's ice-blue eyes. "You're the son of King Markdor and Queen Calla and second in line to the throne. I think you're a tad more aristocratic than me, but I see your point."

"Tordor is second in line to the throne," Latimus said with a firm nod. "Thank the goddess my brother did his kingly duty and sired an heir."

"Do you think they will have another? Tordor is no longer a child. Perhaps they both long for more children."

"Perhaps." Latimus's eyebrows drew together as he stared across the sparring field. "Miranda's pregnancy was extremely difficult since Tordor was the first ever Vampyre-Slayer hybrid. She almost died in childbirth, and Sathan is hesitant to put her in danger. But"—he held up a finger—"Miranda wears the pants, so if she says she wants another child, Sathan will have her knocked up before the next sunrise."

"Said by a man desperately in love with his own bonded."

Latimus's lips twitched. "Indeed. I don't even try to deny it anymore. Lila has me in the palm of her hand. I just do what I'm told and try to be the best bonded mate and father so she'll let me keep kissing her. So far, it's working."

Chuckling, Garridan patted Latimus on the shoulder. "Our great and powerful commander, reduced to the whim of a pretty Vampyre aristocrat."

"One with a generous soul and selfless spirit," he said wistfully. "I'll never deserve her, but that's never seemed to bother her. I'm one lucky bastard." Facing Garridan, he asked, "And what of you? I heard rumors you were contemplating asking Celine to bond with you."

Garridan grimaced. "Did you happen to hear that from Father? He's been hounding me to settle down for centuries. Aristocrats rarely become soldiers, but I always felt a calling to fight, even when I was young. Since I'm second-born and my brother performs our formal duties, Father let me train. I think your position as commander was helpful in that decision."

"I'm thankful he allowed you to join the army. You're one of my most cunning and loyal soldiers."

"And I'm pretty good at combat, I think?" he joked, rubbing his chin.

Latimus breathed a laugh. "You are. We've fought so many skirmishes side by side. Thank the goddess the War of the Species ended and we vanquished Crimeous. Once Bakari is defeated, we will hopefully secure peace for the immortal world. Do you wish to wait to settle down until our conflict with him is over?"

Garridan kicked the ground with the toe of his black boot and shook his head. "I'm not in love with Celine," he said softly. "She is a wonderful female and should bond with someone who can love her in all the ways she deserves."

Latimus's brows lifted. "I see. Does this mean you're in love with someone else?"

Pursing his lips, Garridan gazed over the broad field, his eyes landing on the woman who consumed his every thought. She was sparring with Cian, expertly wielding her sword as the much larger male attempted to fight her off. White fangs glinted in the sun as she sliced and swung the weapon through the air, the metal clanking each time it connected with her opponent's sword.

Garridan had no rhyme or reason for his uncontrollable desire for her. By all accounts, they were opposites in every way. He, the second-born of wealthy Vampyre aristocrats from the sprawling compound of Valeria. She, a feisty lowborn female from a farming village on the outskirts of the laborer compound, Lynia. Her firm, curvy body and broad shoulders were perfect for carrying the bales of corn her father harvested from the fields that surrounded her small family home. She'd told him of it once, when they'd had a small moment of reprieve—and when she'd somehow forgotten, if only for a short time, that she detested him.

"Ah," Latimus said, slowly nodding. "I see."

"It is nothing," Garridan said, straightening his spine. "Siora is just another soldier to me."

Silence stretched between them before Latimus cupped his shoulder. "My friend, you are a terrible liar."

He scoffed and elicited a sigh. "Siora seems to think I'm a misogynistic snob who doesn't believe women deserve a place in our army."

"That's not even close to true," Latimus said, bristling. "You were one of the first to support allowing females to join the combat troops. Where did she obtain that notion?"

"She is a talented soldier, and I push her. She finished a clear and resounding third place in all the physical trials we've held over the past week and finished first on the written exam. There is no doubt she will secure one of the squadron leader positions."

"Our first female squadron leader," Latimus said, reverence in his tone. "My mother would be proud."

"Yes. Siora thinks I single her out because she is a woman, but that isn't true. She has the potential to become a multi-squadron lieutenant one day, and I push her because I want her to excel. But she's exceedingly stubborn and often antagonistic, which I see as her greatest drawback."

"Perhaps she is antagonistic because she desires you as well."

"I never said I desire her," Garridan muttered.

Latimus gave him a droll look. "You didn't have to."

Sighing, Garridan rubbed his hand over his face. "Desire has no place in our army or the conflict with Bakari. I will train her and help her succeed, and then she will become squadron leader. That is my main focus. I'm tired of being consumed by war and wish for our people to live in peace."

"As do I, my friend. Hopefully, it will happen in the upcoming battle. I'm going to join the troops in their sparring session. Want to join me?"

"I'll stay here and continue observing. I'll record my notes this evening before heading home. We should be able to announce the new battalion leaders next week."

"Fantastic," Latimus said, fangs flashing as he gave a salute and began trudging down the hill.

"Don't let Cian kick your ass again!" Garridan teased, chuckling when Latimus lifted his fist and extended his middle finger as he trailed toward the troops.

Glancing at Siora again, he noticed she had knocked the weapon from her sparring partner's hand and now held the tip of her sword against his neck, waiting for him to call mercy. Damn, she was fierce. Tamping down his admiration, he reminded himself he needed to focus on observing *all* the soldiers, not just the one who always drew his gaze with her masterful skill, gorgeous body, and piercing ice-blue gaze.

S iora gritted her teeth, thrusting her sword into her opponent's chest before he grunted and backed away.

"Damn it, Siora," Cian said, holding his hand to his chest. "That fucking hurt."

"You're wearing protective gear," she said, scowling. "You struck me just as hard in the side, and I didn't even wince."

"Maybe you're tougher than me," he said, still rubbing his chest as he grinned, "or maybe you don't have the ability to hit like a girl."

"Hit like a girl, my ass," she muttered, tossing her sword to the ground before picking up the container to chug some much-needed water. Wiping her mouth with the back of her arm, she sighed. "I've never hit like a girl."

"Truer words."

Latimus approached, calling all the troops together and informing them they would spar another hour before heading home. Siora glanced at the sun, noting it was still looming above the horizon, and was pleased she'd have time to help her father at the farm before darkness settled in.

"You're doing very well, Siora," Latimus murmured, and she turned to stare into his sky-blue eyes. "I have no doubt you will become a battalion leader before the final battle with Bakari. After we win, you can have your choice of assignments, whether it be field-based or tailored toward security. I still plan to maintain an army, although it hopefully won't need to be as formidable since we will finally be at peace."

"I love combat," she said, lifting a shoulder. "There's something cathartic about kicking someone's ass."

Chuckling, he gave a nod. "That there is. Keep excelling, and you could become head of security at one of the compounds. That should keep you busy."

"Lynia is my home, so that's where I'd like to be stationed regardless of which position I attain. I'll do my best to earn it."

"I have no doubt." Lifting his brows, he asked, "Want to spar with this old man?" He pointed his thumbs at his chest. "I'm feeling the need to expend some energy."

Siora couldn't contain her smile. A request from the powerful commander to spar with him in front of the troops was an honor and would help cement her status as a competent soldier. The army had only recently allowed women to join the combat troops, and she felt an intense obligation to prove the decision was warranted.

"I'm not going to go easy on you," she said, arching a brow.

"I'd be disappointed if you did." Striding toward the weaponry rack, Latimus selected a sword. Soldiers milled around, gathering to watch the impending showdown.

Lifting her sword, Siora crouched and pointed it straight at his chest. "Ready when you are."

He settled into position before charging, and she felt the magnificent surge of adrenaline she always felt when an impending challenge occurred. Then, she swung her sword through the air, thrilled when the metal clanked against the commander's, and got down to the task of kicking his ass.

Chapter Two

S iora arrived home that evening as the sun lingered over the far-off mountains, a bright, orange orb in the graying sky. Tossing her bag on the porch, she headed behind their small two-bedroom house to the fields lined with corn. Her father was hunched over, picking the husks and depositing them in his basket.

"Hey, Dad," she said, her tone soft so she wouldn't startle him. "Want me to help? I can grab a basket from the shed."

"Hi, sweetie," he said, rising and extending his hands. Grasping them, she placed a kiss on his forehead. "I'm almost finished, but thank you. The harvest has been good this year. Thank the goddess for the growing population of hungry Slayers and Deamons on our tiny compound. I've been selling out at my booth every week-end. The reconciliation of the species has been fantastic for business."

"Better than all the centuries harvesting corn for the Slayers imprisoned at Astaria, that's for sure. Maybe we'll make enough to actually build the annex onto the house this year."

"I think we might," he said, light blue eyes the mirror image of hers sparkling in the rays of the lowering sun. "Your mother would be proud."

"I'd like to think so," she said, sifting the toe of her boot through the tilled dirt. "I still remember her singing to me all those years ago, before she was slain in the Awakening."

"Goddess, but she had a beautiful voice," he said wistfully, briefly closing his eyes. "You were the light of our lives. Our little Siora."

"And then I became your big Siora," she teased, lifting her arms. "I think I'm a head taller than you, Dad."

"You have the constitution of a warrior. I have no idea where it came from, although your mother's brother was a fine soldier, Etherya bless his soul." He laid his hand over his heart. "I miss both of them terribly."

Siora's eyes darted between his. "Would you consider bonding again? If I continue to excel in the army, it's possible I'll have to move closer to the main castle at Lynia's town square if I get promoted. I don't want you to be alone."

"It's only a forty-minute walk into town," he said, waving his hand, "and I know my daughter will come to visit me."

"I will, and I can also teach you to drive a four-wheeler."

"None of that," he said, shaking his head. "I'm not interested in the human technology you soldiers toy around with. I have two working legs, and they can carry me into town just fine."

Chuckling, Siora tilted her head. "You know, I'm pretty sure I get my stubborn streak from you. It runs pretty deep."

"Then I am proud," he said, lowering to pick up the basket full of corn. "It is a noble quality no matter how badly your mother used to tease me for it. One must stand by their convictions."

Siora reached over and tugged the basket from his hands, settling it on her hip as he emitted a huff.

"I can carry it, dear."

"Let your daughter help you. You've worked all day."

They trailed toward the home, Siora placing the basket in the shed before locking it.

"I'll get to shucking them in the morning," he said. "Let's have dinner. I've got some Slayer blood ready, and Ophelia dropped off some nice wine she picked up in town."

Grinning at the mention of their neighbor, who Siora suspected had a crush on her dad, she cupped his shoulder. "She's a nice woman, Dad."

"She is," he said, climbing the wooden steps to enter their home. "I wasn't sure when Queen Miranda and King Sathan decreed reformed Deamons could live on our compounds, but she is lovely."

"You could take a day off and escort her into town for one of the street fairs."

"Stop trying to matchmake, girl," he said, shooing her with his hand. "I'm too old for that nonsense."

"You're never too old—"

"Enough," he interrupted. "We should be discussing finding a mate for *you.*"

Rolling her eyes, she huffed. "Thanks, but I'm all set. I told you, I like being single."

Curiosity entered his gaze. "Don't you want someone to come home to after your long days of training to protect our world? Don't you want to give your father some grandbabies?"

"Oh, brother," she muttered. "We've officially entered the uncomfortable portion of the evening. Come on—let's table this and have dinner and wine. That should take your mind off grilling me."

They trailed inside, her father dismissing the subject for now, but Siora knew it would rear its head again. Reminding herself that he loved her and wanted what he thought was best, she let the conversation go.

Siora had never longed for a partner or to have kids. Was she against it? Not really. But being a plain, stocky girl who'd grown into a brawny, intimidating woman didn't really appeal to men in her experience. She wasn't biddable or coy or whatever the hell Vampyre males wanted in their mates. Although the immortal world had evolved somewhat from its stuffy, traditional history, it still remained quite staid in her opinion. Now she was a warrior in the army and that only decreased her chances of finding a mate.

In her experience, Vampyre males wanted soft, wispy women who would giggle and bat their eyelashes as they flirted. Siora had never flirted in her damn life and had no reason to start now. She could never fake being someone she wasn't. It just wasn't in her DNA.

She liked being tough and was pretty sure she would one day become the highest-ranking female officer in the immortal army if she kept up her grueling training. No one knew she woke up at 4:00 a.m. every day and trained an extra two hours before reporting to duty. She was determined to be as formidable as any man on the field—*more* formidable if she had her way—no matter the energy she had to expend.

There was honor in that, and it satisfied her more than any man ever could.

Even General Garridan...

Gritting her teeth at the words as they silently flitted through her brain, she squeezed her lids shut, trying to rid her mind of the image of his strikingly handsome face. Deep amber eyes stared back at her, refusing to vanish no matter how hard she tried. His fangs glistened atop his full lower lip in her vision, above strong shoulders and a chiseled chest. The aristocrat towered over her, which had always been disconcerting. Very few men made her feel small, but the infuriating general certainly did. If he wanted to envelop her in his thick arms and tug her head back to claim her lips, he could overpower her in a second...

"Dear?" her father asked, perplexed as he held up two goblets. "Ready for dinner?"

"Yes," she uttered, frustrated she was daydreaming *yet again* about the asinine general's kiss. The visions had become more frequent lately, especially since he sparred shirtless around the troops. How was her brain supposed to function when he bared that magnificent chest at every opportunity?

"Bastard."

"Who is?" her father asked.

Damn, she'd said it out loud. Sighing, she shook her head and sat at the small table, grasping the goblet of Slayer blood and lifting it high. "No one. To another great harvest. Congrats, Dad. It's going to be a good year."

Clinking his glass with hers, his eyes sparkled. "It certainly is."

Settling in to the lovely meal with her favorite person on the planet, Siora tried to push thoughts of Garridan from her mind while inwardly admitting the task was futile.

Garridan scowled behind the wheel of the utility vehicle as he approached his home at Valeria. It sat beside his parents' austere mansion but wasn't as large. They'd given him the plot of land centuries ago, hoping he would build a home, settle down with a bonded mate, and have children. Well, one out of three wasn't bad, he guessed.

His father sat on the porch, his face an impassive mask as always. Turning off the four-wheeler, Garridan stepped from the vehicle and approached.

"Hello, Father. I expected you to already be at dinner with Mother and Sebastian."

"Sebastian was held up at the governor's mansion and won't make dinner tonight. It afforded me the opportunity to speak to you."

Lowering into the chair opposite his father, Garridan eyed him warily. "If you're looking to argue, I'm exhausted and would rather wait until I have the energy."

Astaroth's eyes narrowed. "Don't be antagonistic. This will only take a moment, but it's important."

"Okay."

"Would you like to go inside?"

"It's a nice evening," Garridan said, relaxing in the chair. In truth, he cherished his space and didn't want his father's toxic energy inside his home. "Let's chat here."

"Very well." Lacing his fingers, he rested his hands in his lap. "There is a fundraiser in two weeks as the king and queen are looking to raise money for the army. It will be held in the main ballroom at Valeria's governor's mansion."

"Good," Garridan said with a nod. "The new TECs are expensive, and it will be nice for the aristocrats to contribute to the cause."

"As opposed to you, who contributes with brawn and sweat. I am still frustrated you donated your entire trust to the immortal army. I can't fathom how you exist on a soldier's salary."

"This land you gave me was all I needed," he said, gesturing with his hand. "I have a home and a job I love. Wars are expensive, and we must win them if you want to keep living your lavish lifestyle."

"Don't mock me. You are still the beneficiary of much privilege as my son."

"I know," he said, softening his tone. "I appreciate what you and mother have done for me. I'm sorry you don't understand my choices. We've been doing quite well at agreeing to disagree, haven't we?"

His father's lips twitched. "We have, but I fear that might soon change."

Garridan's eyebrows lifted. "Because?"

Silence stretched between them before he spoke. "Because I have promised Handor you will accompany Celine to the fundraiser as her escort."

Grimacing, he shook his head. "No. It's possible I won't even be available that evening. The training sessions are becoming more intense as we near the final battle with Bakari."

"Son," Astaroth said, leaning forward, "when the battle is over and the immortals win by the grace of Etherya, you will have no place as a soldier. It will be time to resume your aristocratic duties. Time to find a mate and settle down. Celine would be a fine choice."

"Celine is a lovely woman, but she is not my mate," he said with finality. "And I will still remain in the army in some capacity. I love it too much to leave."

"Ridiculous," he spat, sitting back and huffing in frustration. "You have a duty!"

"Duty is what we make of it, Father." Running a hand through his thick, dark hair, he sighed. "I won't let you push me into a life I don't want. I'm sorry."

Rising, his father's thin body vibrated with anger. "You know nothing of duty," he said, jabbing a finger in his face. "Nothing of what it means to uphold your aristocratic obligation with honor!"

"Don't yell at me," Garridan said, rising to his full height, several inches above his father. "I don't want to argue. Focus on Sebastian if you must. Perhaps you can 'save' one of your sons from ruin," he said sardonically, making quotation marks with his fingers.

"Sebastian is another story, and I won't let you change the subject. At least he sits on the council and fulfills his aristocratic obligation. You both need to bond with an honorable female, but he does not shirk his duty."

"You have some nerve to say I shirk duty when I've fought by Commander Latimus's side for centuries. Go home to mother. I'm done with this conversation." Dismissing him, he began to walk toward the front door.

His father grabbed his arm, causing him to whirl around, and anger simmered in his gut.

"I will donate the funds to Queen Miranda for her to purchase a thousand additional TECs for the final battle *if*"—he lifted a finger—"you escort Celine to the fundraiser in two weeks' time. If not, you can explain to the queen why I have withdrawn my donation."

"That's absurd. Defeating Bakari will help solidify your safety as well. You're drowning in money and will barely miss the donation."

"I've made my decision," he said, slicing a hand through the air. With a final nod, he began trudging down the stairs. "I would like an answer tomorrow so I can confirm to Celine's father you will accompany her. Good night, son. I won't tell your mother of your disparagement of our heritage. It would break her heart."

Garridan watched him stalk away with slitted eyes, furious at being manipulated with the one thing he loved most: protecting his people. Wondering for the millionth time how he was related to someone so cold and unyielding, Garridan muttered to himself as he unlocked the door and stepped inside.

After a warm shower and much contemplation, he sat down to enjoy his dinner of Slayer blood and wine. Furious, he admitted he would accompany Celine to the fundraiser because his men needed all the extra weapons they could get.

"Your *soldiers* need all the weapons they can get," he murmured in a self-deprecating tone, acknowledging Siora would shoot him a hate-filled glare if he called the troops "men."

He'd done it a few times in front of her—out of habit and certainly unconsciously—and she'd raked him over the coals for it each time.

Feeling the corner of his lips curve, he acknowledged how much he cherished her furious scolding. Hell, he actually longed for it. She would stare up at him with those gorgeous eyes, spittle flying between her fangs as she laid into him. Sometimes, she would even shove him or punch his arm before he gave her a look of warning, reminding her he was her superior. Her glorious features would form a scowl under her short cap of black hair, and she'd grunt before walking away, muttering to herself what an ass he was.

Would she grunt like that if he returned her touch? If he drew her toward him and fashioned those full red lips into some action other than scolding him? Perhaps kissing him with fervor, as he longed to do to her, or placing the plump flesh over other parts of his body...

Glancing down, Garridan grimaced at the erection now tenting his sweatpants. All it took was one thought of Siora's gorgeous lips, and he was hard as a damn rock. Deciding he needed a release, he slid his hand beneath the waistband, gripping his turgid cock as he groaned.

"Siora," he whispered, sliding his hand back and forth over the sensitive flesh, imagining it was her hand...her lips...her *tongue*...

And then, he closed his eyes, allowing himself to fully succumb to the vivid dream he wished was reality.

Chapter Three

T he next day, Siora sparred with one of the new recruits from Naria as Garridan and Latimus observed. The new soldier, Kristoff, was skilled and quick as a damn jackrabbit. Every time she tried to gain the upper hand, he anticipated her strike. Frustrated, she gave a grunt and thrust her weapon. He knocked it to the ground and promptly held his blade to her neck, causing her to curse.

"You're dropping your hip, Siora," Garridan's deep voice boomed from several feet away. "It's a tell, and that's how Kristoff keeps gaining the advantage."

"I'm doing nothing of the sort," she gritted, knocking Kristoff's weapon away with her arm. "Get that thing away from me. You won this skirmish. I concede." The words tasted like gravel on her tongue, but she figured they were the fastest way to get everyone's attention off her and back to something else so she could lick her wounds.

"You'll need to remedy your weaknesses if you want to become a battalion leader," Garridan said. "Not to mention, it will come in handy against Bakari's Deamon soldiers."

"Thanks, Captian Obvious," she said, rolling her eyes before giving him a scowl. "I've been training in my father's fields for centuries, waiting for the time you cavemen would let women into the army. I think I've got this."

"Take five," Latimus commanded to Kristoff and the other nearby soldiers, although his gaze was firm on Siora's. "We'll resume after you all grab some water across the field." The soldiers dispersed while Siora held firm, understanding the commander was displeased with her.

"I'm sorry," she said, lowering her gaze and kicking the ground. "I got frustrated."

"I understand," Latimus said, approaching her. Garridan followed close behind, and she felt the annoying sting of tears behind her eyelids. The last thing she wanted was for the handsome soldier she claimed to detest to see her vulnerable.

Straightening her spine, she cleared her throat. "It won't happen again."

"You are a natural leader, Siora," Latimus said, compassion and firmness in his tone. "But you cannot disrespect General Garridan. He is your commanding officer and has earned the respect that entails."

Feeling like a scolded child, she nodded. "I'm sorry, General Garridan."

Garridan shot Latimus a look before those deep amber eyes locked onto hers. "You almost sound contrite. Good job, Siora."

Her chin jutted forward. "Don't placate me! You've observed the soldiers sparring for two hours on this field, and I'm the only one you've critiqued!"

"Siora—" Latimus said.

"It's okay," Garridan interjected, showing his palm. "She's right." Facing her, he tilted his head. "I called you out because I see the most potential in you, Siora. You are already an excellent soldier, but there is another level you can attain. I push you because I believe in you."

Feeling her eyebrow arch, she placed her hands on her hips. "Or because I'm a woman, and you think I'm not capable."

A wounded expression crossed his features before it vanished, and guilt welled in her chest. Damn it. Now, she felt like a jerk.

"I know I've slipped up since females joined the army, and I'm working on that, Siora. I've been a soldier for centuries in a male-dominated army. It would be nice if you could cut me some slack."

Wanting to be done with the annoying and uncomfortable conversation, she gave a nod. "Fine. I'll work on not dropping my hip. I have to work ten times as hard to excel, and even with that effort, I make mistakes I'm not even aware of. It's infuriating. I apologize for taking it out on you."

His eyes darted over her face. "I could help you...if you'd like. No obligation or pressure. We already work long hours as it is."

"What do you mean?" she asked, eyes narrowing.

He shrugged. "I can have some sparring sessions with you early in the morning, or after our daily training, where we work on ensuring you don't drop the hip. I think I can help since I've observed you in several sparring sessions."

"That's an excellent idea," Latimus said. "I want you to be our first female battalion leader, Siora. You've worked hard for it, and you deserve it. Plus, it will make my feminist sister-in-law and her hardheaded sister happy," he said, referencing Queen Miranda and Governor Evie. "Any opportunity to improve your skills only helps get you to that position faster."

Swallowing thickly, Siora contemplated. She couldn't tell them she already got up early to perform extra training each morning. It was something she didn't want anyone to know, lest they perceive her needing the extra conditioning as a weakness. Still, she saw the merit in Garridan's offer.

"I can only do evenings," she said, her voice gruff although she didn't know why. It certainly had nothing to do with the fact she was about to sign up for private sparring sessions with the hottest Vampyre she'd ever met. Nope. Not at all.

"Evenings are fine," he said with a nod. "We can use the indoor facilities at Lynia's training center."

It rarely rained in the immortal world. Many credited their revered goddess Etherya, who they believed blessed them with warm, sun-kissed days. However, each compound in the immortal world had an indoor training center for the days it did rain, designed by Kenden, the brave and cunning Slayer commander, and built by laborers from Naria, Lynia, and Restia.

"Okay," she said, nodding. "I appreciate the offer. Should we start this evening?"

"I have a commitment this evening, but tomorrow evening works. We can pick up some Slayer blood along the way and ingest it before we begin our training."

Curiosity threatened to choke her as she wondered what his plans were this evening. Did they involve Celine? She'd heard various rumors Garridan would bond with the aristocrat after the final battle with Bakari. Siora had observed Celine a few times, mostly when she'd been tasked with delivering various firearms and weapons to the soldiers who guarded Valeria's large castle. Celine frequented the castle since she was good friends with the governor's daughter, and Siora admitted the woman was exceedingly gorgeous.

She had long, flaxen hair that flitted in the breeze, and she seemed to walk as if she was in slow motion. Her frame was willowy and always covered with the flowing, regal gowns many aristocratic women still insisted on wearing even though their kingdom had become more modernized over the past decades. Glancing down at her own tactical gear—black cargo pants, a T-shirt, and dirt-stained boots—Siora admitted she and Celine were polar opposites.

The woman was a tiny wisp of a thing, whereas Siora was thick and brawny. There wasn't a feminine curve on her, nor was there an undefined muscle. She was sinewy and strong, and she damn well liked it that way. Garridan might covet a porcelain beauty like Celine, and that was just fine, because it added yet another reason to the ten thousand others tallied in her head as to why she needed to squelch her unwanted attraction to the general.

"Siora?"

"Tomorrow's fine," she said, lifting her chin. "Thank you, General Garridan. Hopefully, I can learn quickly, and we'll only need a few sessions."

Something unreadable flitted across his face before he spoke. "I'll do my best. It's a pretty bad tell."

Biting the inside of her cheek, she resisted the urge to tell him to stuff it before catching Latimus's almost inaudible chuckle.

"I think he's joking with you, Siora."

"I am," Garridan said, smiling. By the goddess, the gesture transformed his features into something so sexy her damn knees felt weak. When had she become one of the simpering women she professed to hate? Good. Fucking. Grief.

"Maybe we'll even become friends as we spar," he continued, arching a brow.

"I don't need any more friends," she said, although the statement rang false. In truth, her friends were comprised of the other soldiers, especially Jack, Latimus's son, and his friend Brecken, both of whom she held great affection for. Other than that, her best friend in the world was her father. Which was pretty fucking lame. Sighing, she shook her head. "But I'm sure it will make me detest you less. That's a good start."

Amusement entered his amber gaze along with a slight twinge of mirth, and she damn near fainted. What were women supposed to do when the man they'd had a multitude of unwanted lust-filled dreams about looked them straight in the eye like that? Clenching her thighs together, she commanded her body to stay calm. Vampyres had a heightened sense for arousal, and if she grew slick from his searing gaze, he would certainly smell it.

"I look forward to the opportunity to make you like me, if only a little." He held his thumb and forefinger an inch apart. "On that note, I'm going to grab some water before we resume." Pivoting, he sauntered toward the soldiers who stood by the far-off replenishment station, his broad shoulders beckoning to her.

"He believes in you, Siora," Latimus said, palming her shoulder. "Someone of his rank doesn't have to dedicate one-on-one time to training a cadet."

"I know, and I'm grateful," she said, feeling her throat bob. "I'll make an effort to do better with him. I have a rather large chip on my shoulder, in case you didn't notice. You all kept us out of the army for a long fucking time, Commander."

"We did," he said, grimacing. "Believe me, Miranda and Evie have raked me over the coals extensively for that oversight. Having you and the other fifty women in this first batch of recruits has only made us better. I look forward to the day when our army is comprised equally of men and women."

"Me too. Thank you for believing in me. I won't let you down."

"I know you won't. Now, I know you're a super soldier compared to the rest of us, but I need some water. Come drink some with me so I don't feel bad."

With a grin, she fell into step beside him, pushing away her reservations about training with Garridan. She would plow through them like she always plowed through tough situations, and it would ultimately make her a better soldier. Focusing on the positives, she replenished her electrolytes, ready to embark on the next round of training.

Chapter Four

G arridan found Celine that evening in the fragrant gardens surrounding the massive governor's castle at Valeria. He'd quickly headed home and showered after finishing with the troops and felt it imperative to speak to her regarding the upcoming fundraiser. She was friends with Governor Camron's daughter, Hilara, and could often be found at the mansion.

"General Garridan," Celine said, rising from the stone bench beside a row of green bushes. "How lovely to see you."

"Hello, Celine," he said with a courteous nod. "And hello, Hilara. You both look like you're enjoying the nice weather before the sun sets."

"We are," Hilara said, rising, "but it's almost time for dinner. You'll call me later, Celine?"

"Yes," she said as her straight blond hair flitted in the breeze. "Have a good evening."

"May I escort you home?" Garridan asked, offering his arm as Hilara waved before heading back toward the mansion.

"You may, sir." Her tone was teasing as she placed her arm in his, and they began to stroll past the soldiers who lined the path, ensuring the safety of the governor's family. "I assume you want to speak about the fundraiser."

"Yes," he said, hoping the conversation didn't become uncomfortable. He'd always liked Celine, and although it wasn't a love match, he didn't want to hurt her feelings. "Our fathers are intent on matchmaking. Although we come from traditional families, I rather thought they would see the benefit of us choosing our own bonded mates."

Blue eyes sparkled as she grinned. "So you do not desire to sweep me off my feet? My heart is broken." She placed a hand over her chest.

"I hope you're joking," he said as they trailed onto the sidewalk lining the two blocks that led to her family's large home. "If not, I might be the cad my father accuses me of being."

Chuckling, she shook her head. "You are wonderful, Garridan, truly. But..."

"Yes?"

"I...well, this is hard to say out loud." Clearing her throat, she said, "I fear I love another. Or, at least, I *think* I do."

Curiosity coursed through him. Celine usually wore a polite expression that showed nothing of her feelings—a manifestation of her strict aristocratic upbringing. He'd never seen one hint of desire or longing on her pretty features.

Unable to squelch the curiosity, he asked, "Anyone I know?"

White fangs squished her lip as she gazed up at him, contemplating. "Hilara is the only other one who knows. I don't want to tell anyone else, lest it start an untoward rumor. Regardless, he does not return my affection, so it matters naught."

"I find that hard to believe, Celine," he murmured. "You are one of the most beautiful women in our kingdom and would make a wonderful bonded mate."

"To everyone but you," she chided, amusement in her eyes.

"I would not make you happy. I'm a brute who enjoys war and combat. You'd do better with someone more refined like Sebastian."

She tensed for a brief moment, and realization slammed through him.

"By the goddess, is it Sebastian you have feelings for?"

She quickly shook her head. "Of course not. He's a proclaimed bachelor, and I have it on good authority he asked Mila to accompany him to the fundraiser."

Smiling, Garridan inwardly acknowledged his brother's cleverness. They'd known Mila since they were children as her family's estate bordered their own. The three of them were close, which meant Garridan and Sebastian knew secrets Mila kept close to her heart—the most closely guarded one being that she preferred women to men.

In their provincial kingdom, Mila had guarded the secret for centuries, enjoying her independence and remaining solo. Now that Queen Miranda and Governer Evie of Takelia had modernized the kingdom, Garridan hoped Mila would one day feel comfortable enough to find a female mate who would make her happy. In the meantime, she and Sebastian had a nice ruse going. They often accompanied each other to functions, ensuring both sets of parents wouldn't meddle or try to match them with an unwanted suitor.

Of course, Garridan would never divulge this information to Celine. It was Mila's to tell, whenever she was ready. But he could at least ease Celine's doubt as to his brother's intentions.

"I assure you, Sebastian is not interested in Mila romantically. They are friends and nothing more."

They halted in front of the black metal gate that arched above the walkway to her home, and she studied him. "How do you know?"

"I just know," he said, dropping his arm to his side once she slid hers away. "Sebastian has no desire to bond right now, which I understand, but when he does, I hope you will not be shy."

Wrinkling her nose, she said, "A proper Vampyre female aristocrat is taught to be soft-spoken and demure."

"Which is rubbish," he muttered. "Our queen does not believe that, and neither should you."

She glanced toward the mansion. "I don't want to embarrass my parents."

"Perhaps asserting yourself could land you a bonded mate they would be proud of. It might be something to think about."

"Perhaps." Lifting to her toes, she gave him a quick peck on the cheek. "Thank you for walking me home. I look forward to accompanying you to the fundraiser."

"As do I. Thank you for understanding. I didn't want to make things awkward."

"Of course not," she said, waving her hand. "I'm not an idiot. I know you don't desire me." Narrowing her eyes, she contemplated. "I think you need someone strong who will challenge you and keep you on your toes. Whoever she is will be very lucky." Lowering into a slight curtsy, she rose and pushed open the gate. "Good night, General Garridan."

"Good night, Celine."

Garridan strode back to the four-wheeler at Valeria, contemplating their conversation. For some reason, he liked the idea of Sebastian courting Celine. His brother would fight it, of course, since he much preferred focusing on his council duties and remaining unattached. But he'd also been drifting like that for years. Hell, they both had in their own ways. Was it time for them to possibly contemplate settling down?

Siora's face appeared in his mind, dirt-stricken and fierce, and he sighed as he slid into the vehicle. Frustrated her image appeared every time he envisioned a bonded mate, he pushed the four-wheeler into gear and drove home, determined to let go of something that could never be. After all, one certainly didn't bond with the person who detested them more than anyone else on the planet. He'd do well to remember that.

Chapter Five

After a grueling day of training, Siora grabbed her pack and slung it over her shoulders, aware of the butterflies that flitted inside her belly. She was nervous as hell to train with Garridan but was determined he would never know. Approaching him where he stood by the four-wheeler, she observed him wave goodbye to Cian before he turned and trotted away.

"Ready?" she asked, unable to control the gravelly rasp in her voice.

"Ready," he said with a nod. "I'll drive us to town to grab some Slayer blood on the way to the training center."

"Cool." She slid into the passenger seat, awareness coursing through her as he folded his large body behind the wheel.

The engine roared to life, and he maneuvered the vehicle to the proper gear. Glancing at his tanned arm, Siora noticed the muscles, strained and sinewy, and licked her suddenly dry lips. Damn it. When did *arms* become sexy? She really needed to get a grip.

He drove to town, where they purchased two portable containers of Slayer blood from the market before proceeding to the training center. They spoke rarely, about their fellow soldiers mostly, but the energy between them wasn't uncomfortable. Instead, she found their moments of silence felt quite...*natural*, which she hadn't expected.

"What's that smirk for?" he asked, his deep baritone lined with amusement.

"I just..." Waving her hand, she searched for the words. "I thought being stuck in a four-wheeler with you would suck, but it's not so bad."

"Why, Siora," he said, resting his hand over his heart, "you have such a way with words."

She punched his arm, causing him to chuckle as he rubbed away the sting. "Ouch. Wait until we start sparring at least."

She'd never seen him like this, more relaxed than when they were training, and it melted something inside she didn't know was frozen. Deciding to roll with the sentiment, she softly uttered, "Thank you."

He glanced over, thick hair ruffling in the wind of the open-topped vehicle, but remained silent.

"For training me," she explained as if he were daft. "You didn't have to. I know I've been a huge bitch to you, and I'm...well, I'm sorry."

Full lips curved into a genuine smile, causing her heart to slam inside her chest. *Keep it chill, Siora*, she inwardly chided. Being friendly was one thing, but she could *not* let her arousal take over. He would smell it in an instant, and she would be mortified, especially since he was all but betrothed to Celine.

"I appreciate the apology, and I'll reciprocate with one." Amber eyes shone in the newly risen moonlight as they approached the training center. "I've fallen into bad habits and needed someone to break me of them. I'm very glad you came along, Siora. Maybe you can rid me of my caveman habits once and for all. Or is it cave*person?*" Parking the vehicle, he rubbed his chin as he stared at the sky.

"Ha ha," she chided, knowing he was making fun of her. "You haven't called the troops 'men' in a while, so I'll let that one go." Jumping out, she slung her bag over her shoulder and fell into step beside him.

Once they were inside, he illuminated the training room, and they walked to the corner where the floor was lined with blue mats.

"I figured we can spar here," he said, pointing to the mats. "They're soft enough that if you throw me on my ass, I'll survive."

"Good, because I'm planning on kicking your ass."

His resulting grin was so sexy she squeezed her thighs together, willing her arousal to stay at bay. "Can't wait."

Setting her bag on the nearby bench, she pulled out the Slayer decanter, drinking before replacing the top. "I'd like to change into yoga clothes if that works," she said, glancing down at her tactical wear. "Better for sparring inside."

"I brought a change of clothes too. Let's change and get to work."

After changing in their respective locker rooms, Siora exited to find him stretching atop the center mat. He was barefoot beneath black sweatpants and a tight black muscle shirt. Although her eyes were dying to glance at the juncture between his thighs—which she *may* have noticed held a significant bulge for the scant moment she assessed him—she aimed her gaze at his stunning eyes and straightened her spine.

"Okay, let's work on this damn dropped hip I can't seem to shake."

Approaching, she stood before him, noticing his eyes dart to the swell of her breasts, pushed high by the sports bra she wore beneath her loose tank top. Suddenly, she felt small in her bare feet beneath her capri yoga pants as he towered above her. The tactical gear she wore on the field added an extra layer that had now been shed. Feeling vulnerable, she glanced toward the weaponry rack that lined the wall, needing a break from his solid gaze.

"Should we grab a sword or sparring stick?"

"Let's give it a go without the weapons first. We'll pretend we have them so your body can move naturally, and I can point out the tell." Crouching, he held up his hands, fisted as if he were holding a sword. "Ready?"

With a nod, she crouched as well, and they got to work. They began a series of sessions where he attacked different parts of her body—shoulder, side, thigh, and so on—so she could analyze where she was dropping her hip. With each new set of motions, she began to understand her weaknesses. Garridan pointed out that she favored her right side, which made sense because she was right-hand dominant. It was something she'd tirelessly worked on in her early-morning sessions during her conditioning. She'd spend countless hours wielding weapons with her left hand to train it to be proficient, but there was only so much one could do when the body was set in its ways.

"No," Garridan said, stepping back and holding up his hands about an hour into their session.

Panting, Siora fisted her hands on her hips and huffed. "I was balancing on my left foot."

"You weren't," he said, shaking his head. "You leaned back on your right foot for leverage before shifting your weight. That's a tell. You have to learn to summon strength without anchoring on your right leg."

Frustrated, she sauntered over to the bench and grasped the water container, angrily chugging before slamming it down. "Damn it. I didn't even feel myself do it."

"That's why we're here," he said, shrugging. "You'll shake the habit with enough practice. Come on. Again." He beckoned to her with his fingers.

Annoyed he was summoning her, she stomped toward him and set her feet. Lifting her hands, she mimicked thrusting a sword, and he charged forward. Attempting to sideswipe his thigh, she shifted her balance, and he landed a soft blow to her back, right above her kidney.

"Fuck!" she yelled, stepping back and rubbing her forehead. "I did it again."

"Come on," he said, encircling her wrist and drawing her back. "Keep going. You're thinking too much."

Annoyance pervaded her veins as they began to spar again, and she reminded herself not to take it out on Garridan. Although his persistence grated on her nerves, he was attempting to help. Her knee-jerk reaction had always been to lash out at him, but *she* was the source of her anger. Hating that she couldn't control her tell, exasperation bubbled within.

"No, Siora!" he said, his tone gruffer than before. "You dropped the hip when I lunged at your side."

"Don't yell at me!" she screamed, unable to control the irritation at her continued failure. "I'm trying—"

"Trying doesn't work in battle," he interrupted, further inflaming her rage. "One false move, and you're dead."

"Why do you care?" she asked, lunging forward to resume their sparring.

Grunting, he blocked her blow and grabbed her wrist, whirling her around so her back slammed into his front. Emitting an *"oomph,"* he slid his arm around her waist, holding her in place so she didn't strike him.

The silken skin of his lips brushed the shell of her ear as he muttered, "Low blow, Siora. You know I wasn't ready—"

She elbowed him in the side, knocking the air from his lungs before trying to spin out of his grasp. Of course, she was no match for his strength and centuries of combined skill. Growling, he swiped her legs, causing her to yelp before she fell to the mat. He tumbled behind, his large body landing atop hers as he cushioned the fall with his arms.

"You son of a bitch," she uttered through clenched teeth, struggling beneath him. Somehow, she managed to turn flat on her back and jutted her fist through the air, determined to knock the fangs straight from his perfect face.

"Damn it!" he gritted before grabbing her wrists and lifting them above her head. Pinning them to the mat, he held them there as he loomed over her, panting and breathless.

Siora struggled, her body wriggling under his, causing him to settle more firmly between her thighs. And then, she felt him against her leg. His hard, throbbing shaft pulsed into the tender flesh through her thin yoga pants, and his grip on her wrists tightened.

Lust blazed in his deep amber gaze before he closed his lids, his body stilling as he seemed to struggle to regain control. His erection pulsed against her skin, beckoning to her body even if her mind wanted no part of it. Knowing she was seconds away from gushing in her damn yoga pants, she emitted a soft whimper.

Those gorgeous eyes slid open and assessed her, the orbs weary but simmering with arousal. Confusion coursed through her as her eyes darted between his. Why was he aroused? Surely not because he was attracted to her. She wasn't beautiful like Celine. Hell, she was light-years from beautiful. Was it just a visceral reaction to a close female body? Of course, that had to be it—right?

"Sorry," he whispered, tongue darting out to bathe his full lips, and she wondered how in the hell she'd somehow entered the most erotic moment of her life. Goddess, but she wanted that tongue on hers, licking and stroking before he trailed it down the smooth skin of her neck and moved lower to lather her nipple...

"You're...aroused," she said, realizing how lame the blatant observation must sound.

A muscle clenched in his jaw as he gritted his teeth. "Yes," he said, contrition in his tone. "I'm sorry. I just need a second. *Fuck...*"

"Why...?" Struggling to find the words, she studied his flushed cheeks and mussed hair. "I'm not... I don't understand."

"You're not what?"

She worked her jaw, trying to find the words. "I'm not...pretty...or womanly...or whatever Celine is."

Breathing a laugh, he shook his head. "You are certainly not what Celine is."

Stiffening, she tried to pull her hands free. "Let me up—"

"Wait," he said, clenching her wrists above her head with one hand as he slowly lowered the other. "That came out wrong." Gently cupping her face, he inched closer. "You aren't what anyone else is, Siora. Don't you know that?" His throat bobbed as he searched her gaze. "You're so much more than anyone I've ever met."

Tears stung her eyes as emotion welled within. "No, I'm not—"

He placed the pad of his thumb over her lips, stopping the words as her body hummed below him. "You *are*," he said, running his thumb across her now quivering lips.

Heat began to curl in every crevice of her body, and she knew hiding her arousal was about two seconds away from being a lost cause. Throwing caution to the wind, she asked softly, "You want me?"

With a harsh laugh, he pushed his erection against her thigh. "I think the answer to that question is obvious." Sliding his hand behind her head, he threaded his fingers through her short hair, gently tugging and urging her closer. The slightly possessive act made something roar inside, and the dam broke free, sending a surge of arousal to her core. Slickness flooded the walls of her deepest place, and his body tensed above her. "The real question is, do *you* want *me?*"

Blood pounded in every cell, preventing her from answering.

"Holy shit," he breathed, closing his eyes and inhaling deeply. Lifting his lids, he stared into her soul. "Goddammit, Siora. Your arousal smells so fucking good."

Shallow breaths mingled with his as her body opened beneath him, inch by slow inch as he settled further between her thighs.

"Yes," she whispered, realizing her body had already accepted the inevitable even if her brain hadn't quite caught up. "I want you."

His fingers tightened in her hair before tugging once again, causing her to purr in anticipation. "If I kiss you, I won't be able to stop there. Do you understand, Siora?"

Nodding, she arched her hips, causing him to hiss.

"You little vixen," he murmured, lowering his head. Touching his lips to hers, he gently brushed them back and forth, driving her wild. "Do you want me to touch you, Siora? Tell me what you want."

"Oh, goddess..." she moaned, undulating beneath him.

"The goddess isn't here, sweetheart," he murmured against her lips, "just you and me. Tell me. I don't want any lingering doubt that we both want this."

"Let go of my wrists," she commanded softly, and he released his grip. Gliding her hands around his neck, she slid them into his thick brown hair. "Garridan, shut the hell up and fuck me."

His resulting smile would've melted her panties if she'd been wearing any underneath her yoga pants. Instead, she grinned back before he slid his lips over hers and consumed her as if she were his last breath.

Chapter Six

Garridan had no idea when he'd become the luckiest son of a bitch on the planet, but he sure as hell wasn't going to squander the moment. Pushing Siora's lips wide with his own, he plunged his tongue inside, tasting her for the first time. She tasted like rain and honey, damp but sweet, and he was overcome by her essence. Her words were direct, which drove him wild, but there was a vulnerability in her embrace, and he longed to earn her trust. Her words about Celine had all but broken his heart, and he would do everything in his power to show her how gorgeous and sexy she was.

Sliding his tongue over hers, he drank her moans, sipping them as he felt her pounding heartbeat beneath his own. Longing to touch her, he broke the kiss, chuckling when she emitted a frustrated whimper.

"Take this off," he murmured, tugging the tank top from her body and tossing it aside. Her pert breasts jutted from the tight sports bra, and his shaft pulsed in response to the trembling globes.

"They're small," she said, glancing down at her breasts, although they looked fine as hell to him. "The bra makes them bigger, I think, because they're all scrunched up in there."

Laughing, he lowered and kissed one of the swells, causing her to toss her head back on the mat and thrust her fingers in his hair. *"Yessss..."* she hissed.

"Is it one of your favorites?" he asked.

"The bra? Not really."

"Good." Gripping the top of the garment with both hands, he ripped it in half. Her pert breasts sprang free, all but popping in his face, and he felt his release pulsing in his shaft. Goddess, he could come just from staring at her sweet, succulent breasts.

With a grunt, he tore the bra from her body and focused on the mounds. Cupping them in his hands, he squeezed, forcing her nipples high. The tight little buds were several shades darker than her pale skin, and he yearned to suck them.

"Garridan," she moaned, spurring joy inside his desire-ravaged frame.

"You sound so sexy when you say my name," he rasped, licking his lips before blowing on one of her turgid nipples. "Say it again."

She complied, sending him to heaven as he lowered his mouth to her breast. He trailed soft kisses around her nipple before nudging it with his nose.

"Look at me."

Those stunning blue eyes lasered into his before he extended his tongue to lick the sensitive bud. Her body bucked, jutting into his erection as he groaned. Gazing into those gorgeous eyes, he closed his mouth around her nipple and began to suck.

"Oh...yesss..." she purred, fingers clenching his hair as she watched him devour her. "That feels so good...oh...*god...*"

"Mmm..." he murmured, knowing the taste of her nipple against his tongue was one of the finest delicacies he would ever savor. He sucked her deep, tugging the sensitive nub, before flicking his tongue against it as she squirmed. Determined to please her, he kissed a path to her other breast and repeated the ministrations, overcome by her tiny mewls.

"Get inside me," she groaned, tugging at his pants while her other hand fisted in his hair. "I need you."

The words sent shivers of pleasure through his frame, and he lifted, yanking off his shirt and pants before dragging off the rest of her clothes.

"I want to make you come first, but I don't know if I can wait—"

"Goddammit, fuck me!" she gritted, frustrated amusement in her tone.

Settling between her thighs, he slid his hand behind her knee and lifted her leg high. "Do you want it hard?"

"Yes!"

Positioning himself, he rubbed the head of his shaft through her slick folds. It felt amazing, and he longed to surge inside her. "Should I grab a condom?"

Vampyres couldn't transmit disease through sex due to their self-healing abilities, but they could still get pregnant.

She shook her head, her short hair fanning across the mat. "Sadie gave me an IUD years ago. I'm set."

Aligning his shaft with her opening, he drew back his hips, ready to claim her. She stared back at him, eyes glazed with lust, and he suddenly understood he needed to slow down. Garridan had fantasized about fucking Siora for months, and he craved her reaction. Pushing her leg high, he began to ease inside.

"Faster," she demanded, and he shook his head as her tight folds enveloped him.

"I need to watch you take me, sweetheart," he murmured, sliding deeper before withdrawing and pushing into her wetness. "You look so pretty."

Confusion entered her gaze as he glided inside, and he was desperate to reassure her. "You have no idea how gorgeous you are. I'm in heaven right now, don't you understand?" Thrusting his hips, he buried himself to the hilt, clenching his teeth as she surrounded his sensitive flesh. "Fuck, you're tight, honey."

"It's been a while."

"Not anymore." Drawing back, he withdrew until only the tip remained inside her sweet body. Steeling himself, he surged inside, the pleasure almost unbearable as her taut channel swallowed him whole. "You're mine now."

"I'm not anyone's—"

Leaning on his forearms, he thrust his fingers in her hair and captured her lips as he began to undulate his hips. Consuming her in a passionate kiss, he began to fuck her in long, hard strokes that set his body on fire.

"Mine," he growled into her mouth, thrilled when she wrapped her leg around his waist, opening her sweet pussy to his invasion.

"Oh, *god,*" she groaned, head tossed back on the mat as she accepted his deep pounding.

Garridan hammered inside, his cock covered with her essence, as she shuddered beneath.

The slickness was everywhere, drenching his aching skin, and he pressed his cheek against hers, needing the connection.

"Can you come like this?"

Shaking her head, she speared her short nails into his back, the pleasure-pain driving him mad. "I need my clit rubbed. It's fine...still feels good...don't stop..."

No way in hell was he going to get off without ensuring she did too. Lifting his hand, he licked his fingers before sliding them between their bodies. Pushing her folds apart, he searched for her sensitive bud as he continued to fuck her. Lifting his head, he assessed her reaction, elated when she gasped.

"Right there," she cried, and he began circling the taut nub of her clit. *"Ohmygod...keep doing that, and I'll fucking explode."*

"Yes," he rasped, his hips now working at a frenzied pace along with his fingers. "Come all over my cock, honey. I want to be covered in your scent. Do you hear me?"

Whimpering, she clenched her arms tighter around his neck, cheeks flushed below her hooded eyes. *"Garridan..."*

Labored breaths exited his lungs as he hammered inside her warmth while beads of sweat formed along his heated skin. They dripped from his chest onto her breasts, coating her as he claimed her, and he felt the primal urge to drink from her. Drinking from another Vampyre was sacred in their culture, and it was usually only done between bonded mates. Still, the longing persisted, and he felt something well deep within. Never had he yearned to drink from a woman during sex, but with Siora...by the goddess, he *craved* it. He ached to feel her blood rush against his tongue as her pussy drenched his cock.

"I'm going to come!" she cried, lips falling open as her mouth formed an "O." "Oh...yes...fuck!"

Her body bowed beneath him, drawing him deeper inside her body as he lunged forward. Lifting his hand from her clit, he slid both palms under her shoulders, anchoring her as he continued to ram inside. Pleasure sparked at the base of his spine as his balls tightened, and he pressed his face into her nape. Clutching her close, he felt the spasms of her orgasm choke his cock in a thousand tiny deaths. Giving into the pleasure, he let go, allowing her tight folds to jerk his release from his cock.

Pressing against her, he moaned her name into the wet skin of her neck as he came. Thick, sticky jets of release shot into her viselike channel, coating her core as the thrill of claiming her deepest place overwhelmed him. Eliciting shouts of bliss, he purged every last drop inside her, wishing he could imprint himself upon her. Her body fit against his as if they were made for each other, and he inwardly laughed at the romantic thoughts. If Siora knew his sappy inner musings, she'd most likely jibe him for it for centuries.

Quakes and shudders wracked his frame until he settled into her, resting his weight on his side so he didn't crush her. Sprawled half-atop her luscious body, he sank into her as she sighed below.

They were tangled together, sweaty and sated, and he nuzzled her as his fingers sifted through her soft, short hair. He knew she wore it that way so she wouldn't have to mess with it during training. It showcased her prominent cheekbones and stunning eyes, which was probably why he caught himself staring at her more often than he should. How could she think Celine was more beautiful? By the goddess, he loved Siora's pretty face and strong features. And her body? It was smooth and powerful, with slight curves in all the right places. To him, she represented true beauty, someone who fought for their people while remaining true to herself. In his eyes, there was nothing more noble.

"You're quiet," she said, running her nails over his back as he shivered. "You're never quiet. Shouldn't you be scolding me? Do you have the urge to point out any tells in my lovemaking?"

Chuckling, he kissed her neck before resting his head on his fist as his elbow dug into the mat. "No complaints here. You were perfect."

Her fangs rested atop her bottom lip as she smiled, making her look adorable—so much softer than she appeared on the field. By the goddess, he wanted to see her like this every day, relaxed and sexy and *open.*

"I did *not* expect that to happen during our training session. I'd apologize, but I think you actually made the first move."

"Why would you apologize for having fantastic sex?" Tracking his finger across her jaw, he regarded her. "Let's do it again next training session."

Joy entered her gaze before she squelched it. "Garridan," she said softly.

"Don't," he whispered, leaning down to kiss her. "Don't take us to the place where we have some serious discussion about whether this was a mistake or not."

"It was."

"Fine," he said, playfully rolling his eyes, "so what if it was? Did you enjoy it?"

"Um, yes," she said, her expression one of mock exasperation.

"Me too. So let's do it again. We have a huge battle before us, and it can't hurt to enjoy ourselves while we work off some steam. I think it will take several more sessions for you to fully let go of your tell. We'll practice each night, and then we'll have sex afterward. It only seems fair." He waggled his eyebrows.

Laughing, she shook her head. "I'm not sure I see the logic, but, hey, you're right about our impending battle. If we're going to die, I'd like to have some magnificent sex before I bite the bullet."

"Exactly." Winking, he smoothed his palm over her shoulder. "No labels, and no serious conversations. We can do all that after the battle, if we both survive."

Her eyes narrowed as she studied him. "I thought you were going to ask Celine to bond with you. The rumor is public knowledge at this point."

Sighing, he shook his head. "My father wants me to marry an aristocrat even though I've told him I have no desire to do so. Celine is a lovely woman, but I don't want an aristocratic life. I enjoy the army and protecting our people."

"That's what I want too. I love being a soldier. It's about time you Neanderthals let us join you."

Feeling his lips curve, his eyes roved her flushed features. "You've taught me a lot. I thought I was so progressive, but I guess you can't see what you've never experienced."

"When I first joined, I couldn't understand why you were so hard on me. I wanted so badly to do well, and I felt like you singled me out."

"I saw your potential from the first day," he murmured, running the backs of his fingers over her cheek. "I knew if I pushed you, you would get better. You might've decided you hate me, but you'd get better."

Her fangs toyed with her lip, causing his shaft to jerk inside her. "I pretty much detested you," she teased. "I was too stubborn to see you were trying to help. And you kept calling us 'men,' which really pissed me off."

"I'm a creature of habit," he said, lifting his shoulder. "I've done better lately, right?"

Nodding, she ran her leg over his hairy one. "You have. I'll try to turn my disdain to something more palatable. Keep fucking me like that, and I'm sure it will happen."

"Mission accepted," he murmured, giving her a peck on the lips. Sighing, he brushed a tuft of hair from her forehead. "I guess we should call it a night."

"Yeah. I want to hang with my dad for a bit before he goes to sleep. We usually have dinner together, but he sees the benefit of my training sessions with you."

"I'd like to meet him one day."

Those stunning eyes widened. "That's definitely moving into 'serious' territory. My dad is my rock. I don't bring home random dudes to meet him."

The challenge swelled in Garridan's chest, and he felt the consuming urge to meet it. One day, he would earn Siora's trust and meet her father. It was a lofty goal for someone as private and guarded as she, and he vowed to make it happen. For now, he gave her a soft smile and arched an eyebrow.

"I'm pretty sure it's insubordination to call your commanding officer a 'random dude,' but I'll let it slide."

Their chuckles filled the room before he helped her to her feet. Once dressed, he drove her home. When they approached the tiny house, he offered to walk her inside, but she declined.

"We're not formal out here on the farm, Garridan," she said, exiting the vehicle and closing the door. "I don't need the red carpet. Thanks for the training, and for...well...thanks."

"You're welcome," he said softly, giving her an informal salute. "See you in the morning."

"See you in the morning." With a wave, she turned to walk up the wooden steps, and he put the car into gear to head home, not giving a damn he wore a perma-grin the entire way.

Chapter Seven

S iora threw herself into training, reminding herself that although it was exhausting, she would have plenty of time to rest after they defeated Bakari. For now, she focused on conditioning her body and mind to excel. She still got up early each day for her solo conditioning, spent several hours on the field, and ended each day with her sessions with Garridan. Most nights, she fell into bed after kissing her father on his bearded cheek and apologizing for not spending more time with him. He would gaze at her with his gentle eyes and tell her how proud he was, which made all the hard work worth it.

Each day on the field, Siora did her best to ensure no one suspected her relationship with Garridan had turned sexual. He treated her the same, still calling her out slightly more than the other soldiers and maintaining it was because he saw her potential. She did her best not to slip into her old pattern of bristling at his coaching, although she sometimes failed. It was on those evenings, after she lost her cool and became frustrated with him on the training field, they ended up having the hottest sex. So, she guessed it wasn't a total failure since it led to such an enjoyable outcome.

"What are you thinking about?" Garridan murmured in her ear, coming to stand behind her as she sipped water on the outer edge of the training field. "You have a shit-eating grin on your face."

Gazing up at him, she almost melted at the desire simmering in his eyes. "I was remembering last night when you punished me for losing my cool on the field yesterday."

His nostrils flared as he emitted an almost imperceptible growl. "I loved bending you over and taking you from behind." His gaze trailed to her breasts, hidden beneath her loose tank top and sports bra. "But taking you from the front is also very enjoyable."

Breathing a laugh, she glanced around the field. "Careful, General. People might begin to suspect something. We can't have that."

He was silent, causing her to stare up at him. He wore an unreadable expression, and it caused nervous butterflies to flit in her stomach.

"Garridan?"

"Right. Don't want anyone to know about our undefined, clandestine affair. Got it."

Latimus summoned them from across the field, and she set her container on the table.

"I think Latimus wants me on the obstacle course."

"I'm working with Cian's group on deploying the new TECs today," he said with a nod. "See you after training. I stocked some Slayer blood in the fridge at the training center, so we can have that before we spar tonight."

"Okay," she said, swallowing thickly as she wondered if she'd somehow upset him. "See you later."

As she jogged to the obstacle course and began the grueling exercise, she couldn't stop her mind from wondering about Garridan's reaction. They'd only been having sex for a few days. It was a casual fling to work off some steam...wasn't it? It wasn't as if they had any sort of a future together once the conflict with Bakari was over. Garridan would most likely assume a high-ranking role in their army while Siora hopefully became head of security at Lynia. Garridan's role would span the entire kingdom, so he'd most likely be stationed at one of the more prominent compounds, while Siora had no desire to live anywhere but Lynia. Her father lived there, and she would always choose to live nearby so he wouldn't be alone.

Although Garridan claimed to have no desire to bond with an aristocrat, it was very unlikely he would consider bonding with her. The scandal of a high-ranking Valerian aristocrat of Garridan's prominence bonding with the daughter of a Lynian farmer would send shock waves through Valerian society. Although the kingdom had evolved from the strictest adherences to tradition since Miranda became queen, there were limits to the progressiveness. Hell, Garridan's parents would most likely disown him if they knew he'd even touched a poor farmer's daughter from Lynia.

Still, knowing all that, Siora wouldn't lie to herself. As she maneuvered her body across the obstacle course, daydreams flashed through her mind. Ones of her and Garridan working together to secure the kingdom by day and heading home together at night. To a shared home where her father was waiting and tiny Vampyres with Garridan's amber eyes and thick brown hair ran to them with open arms. In her vision, she embraced the tots before settling in for dinner and eventual sleep. Then, once the house was quiet, he would hold her as they recounted stories from their day before making passionate love and falling asleep wrapped in each other's arms.

"What the fucking hell?" she muttered to herself, grunting as she scaled the rock wall that lined the obstacle course. "Ditch the daydreams, Cinderella."

"You talking to yourself, Siora?" Radomir chided as he climbed beside her. "Keep it up so I can kick your ass."

"In your dreams, buddy," was her confident reply before she high-tailed it over the summit and scaled down the opposite side. Once on the ground, she disengaged from the rope and wiped the dirt from her hands.

"Damn, you're fast," Radomir said, landing beside her and unclasping the hook that held his rope. "It's a good reminder not to jibe you. Just makes you more likely to beat me." He tapped his temple before pivoting and heading toward the cooler that held fresh canisters of water.

"Get your fucking mind out of la-la land, Siora," she scolded, kicking the dirt with the toe of her boot. Fantasizing about any sort of future with Garridan was futile and an extreme waste of time. They were just fucking, and when their one-on-one sessions were over, their trysts would end too. The thought flooded her with a thousand tiny prickles of sadness, but she lifted her chin, determined to push them away.

And when in the hell had she started visualizing having children? For the goddess's sake, she'd never dreamed of having kids with anyone. She wasn't opposed, necessarily. It just didn't seem like something one did when their primary goal was to excel as a soldier. If she chose that path, she would need a partner who understood her desire to balance her military career *and* motherhood, which was extremely hard to find in a society where women had only recently obtained the ability to join the army.

But Garridan would understand...

The words floated through her brain before she could stop them, and she waved her hand, somehow attempting to shoo them away although it was pointless. They lingered deep within, forcing Siora to acknowledge they were true. Garridan was perhaps one of the only men on the planet who would support her military aspirations and wish for her to succeed. He was invested in ensuring it happened, and there was a nobility in that, which made the complex emotions she experienced around him even more confusing.

"Great job, Siora," Latimus said, approaching. "You were the fastest on all the obstacle course challenges today. I'm excited to announce it to the entire regime later."

Pride swelled within that her early-morning conditioning exercises were paying off. "Thank you, Commander. I want to do well so I can lead a battalion when we face Bakari."

"I've been thinking about that," he said, tilting his head. "You and Garridan have been getting along in your one-on-one sessions, right?"

If he only knew. "Yep," she said, feeling like a dolt at the overly cheerful tone of her voice. *Keep it cool, Siora. Good grief.* "I've learned so much from him. He's extremely skilled at one-on-one combat."

"Good. I've been thinking about the battle, and I want you two to team up and lead three battalions. He will be commanding officer, but you'll be second-in-command. If all goes well, it's a natural step toward your progression in the army. Afterward, if we win—"

"*When* we win," she said, lifting a finger.

"When we win," he said with a grin, "I'll speak to Commander Kenden and nominate you for head of security at Lynia. After co-leading a successful mission with Garridan, it should be a no-brainer."

Elation bloomed in her chest, and she couldn't contain her smile. "That would be amazing. I'll lead the troops with everything I have and will work with General Garridan to ensure we remain as safe as possible while kicking Bakari's ass."

"Excellent. In the meantime, keep it up on the obstacle courses and in the training sessions. Cian and Radomir still have the edge on you in sparring history. Hopefully, you'll close the gap as you learn to hide your tells."

"I will." Straightening, she puffed out her chest. "I'm determined to even the score, believe me."

Chuckling, he cupped her shoulder. "I have no doubt you will. Speaking of, it's time for the afternoon group sparring sessions. You ready?"

Vowing to kick Cian and Radomir's asses no matter how much energy it took, she gave a firm nod. "Ready."

Turning, they headed toward the open meadow, excitement coursing through Siora's veins as she digested the commander's praise.

Chapter Eight

That evening, about an hour into their session, Garridan held up a hand as his full lips formed a smile. "By the goddess, I think we've done it," he said, his words slightly breathless from their exertion.

"Done what?" she asked, straightening from her crouch.

"Fixed your tell. You haven't dropped your hip once today. Well done."

Elation coursed through her. "Sweet. I was hoping I was getting better. It took about a week. Not bad." She patted herself on the back.

Chuckling, he stepped closer and placed his palm over the juncture between her neck and shoulder. "I'm proud of you. I hope that doesn't sound placating or pompous. In the past, I'd probably be afraid to tell you I was proud of you because you'd tell me to shove it."

She gave a playful eye roll. "I wasn't *that* bad."

"Okay," he mocked, scrunching his features.

"It's just different when *you're* different," she said, shrugging. "When you're a woman, and a man in a superior position says he's proud, it indicates surprise. You know, like he had no expectation you could do it in the first place."

His eyes narrowed as he pondered. "I guess that makes sense. It's tough for someone who's never experienced misogyny to put themselves in the shoes of someone who has. But I'm trying, Siora."

"I know," she said softly, sliding her hands over his lower abdomen. He'd ditched his shirt a while ago, and his skin trembled beneath her palms. "You're doing an excellent job, General." Hooking her fingers over the elastic of his sweatpants, she began to ease them down his legs.

"I guess we're done with training," he muttered as she lowered to her knees, dragging his pants to his ankles before urging him to step out and tossing them against the wall. His impressive cock sprung toward her face, already hard and turgid as the veins swelled beneath the sensitive skin.

"Oh, we're done with *training*," she said, arching a brow as she gripped his shaft, "but there will still be *lots* of physical exertion."

"Holy fuck," he breathed, threading his fingers through her short hair and gently clenching. "You have no idea how hot you are kneeling in front of me like that."

"Like this?" she asked, pursing her lips and rapidly blinking. "Or like this?" Lowering her hand, she gripped the hem of her sports bra and tugged it off, tossing it to lie atop his sweatpants. Her breasts sprang free above the yoga pants she still wore, and she felt a moment of self-consciousness. After all, she was stocky and muscular, and her breasts weren't anything to write home about. But Garridan seemed enthralled by them, always spending time on each of her sensitive nipples when they made love, so she figured it wouldn't hurt to bare herself.

"Like that," he growled, inching closer and tilting her head with the fingers entwined in her hair. "Cup them while you suck me."

Grinning, she palmed the small globes in her hands and widened her stance so she could balance more firmly on her knees. Pushing her breasts high, she tilted her head further and opened her mouth.

"You sexy little vixen," he murmured, placing the underside of his cock on her waiting tongue. "Goddess, you're so gorgeous."

"Mmm…" was her sensual response as she closed her mouth around him.

He released a ragged groan as he began to slowly jut back and forth. Staring into his amber eyes, Siora pinched her nipples as she sucked him, sending pleasure through her frame as he loomed above her.

"Yesss..." he hissed, sliding the smooth skin of his shaft across her tongue and lips. "Play with those sexy nipples while I fuck that smart mouth."

Her eyes narrowed, and he breathed a strained laugh.

"Don't give me that look, Siora. You have the smartest mouth I've ever fucking heard. And the sexiest...and the fucking sweetest...oh, *god...*"

Figuring she'd let him off the hook since she enjoyed the spicy compliments, she began to move her head, maneuvering it around his cock as he shoved it inside her willing mouth. Saliva coated the taut skin, making it glisten as he fucked her lips in the quiet room.

"Yeah, honey," he said, his fingers so tight in her hair they sent twinges of pain through her scalp, although they were pleasurable. They were reminiscent of a good workout, where her muscles were tired and sore but endorphins still coursed through her body. Holy shit. Watching Garridan pound her mouth while he gritted his teeth in ecstasy *definitely* sent endorphins through her rapidly heating body.

"Can I move your head?" he asked, making her heart swell. Although she chided him for being an unwitting misogynist, he was a stickler for consent, and damn, if that wasn't sexy as hell. "I don't want to hurt you."

Popping his cock from her mouth, she flashed him a sultry grin. "I'm not some weak aristocrat, Garridan. Pull my hair and fuck my mouth. Use me however you want and come down my fucking throat. Do you hear me?"

A deep growl rumbled in his chest as he yanked her hair. "Goddammit, that's sexy. Say it again."

The corner of her lip curved before she extended her tongue, running it over her top lip and then the bottom one, slow and deliberate. "Garridan? Fuck my mouth. *Hard.*"

Groaning, he complied, sliding his cock between her lips as she closed around him. Gripping her short tresses, he began to fuck her in earnest, plunging toward the back of her throat as she reminded herself to relax. Opening to him, she felt so full when he began to push deep, pulling back so she could suck in breaths between the firm thrusts.

"Do you like swallowing my cock, sweetheart?" he rasped, eyes locked with hers as he possessed every crevice of her mouth. "God, you're driving me wild. Every part of you feels so good."

She purred around his sensitive flesh, wondering when making him feel pleasure became so important to her. Damn, but she craved to hear his deep moans and growls as he loved her. His caresses were always so passionate—and surprisingly tender—and she longed for these nights with him. What would happen now that she'd improved? Would he stop making love to her?

Gliding her hands up his thighs, the tiny hairs prickled her palms as she slid them to his buttocks. Clasping the firm flesh, she helped drive his hips toward her mouth, showing him how much she desired him...hoping he understood she wasn't ready to stop their passionate trysts.

"Fuck!" he gritted, slamming his cock in her mouth. "I'm going to come... Suck me dry, honey...oh...*god...*"

Warm pulses of release began shooting down her throat, and she moaned, closing her eyes as he emptied himself inside her wet mouth. Shouts of pure ecstasy escaped his lungs as his large body pulsed beneath her hands. Spearing her nails in his buttocks, she grinned when he shouted her name.

"You fucking vixen," he groaned, jerking as his body shook from the orgasm. "Damn it, that feels good."

She pushed deeper, knowing he enjoyed the slight pleasure-pain as much as she did, and he shuddered before tugging her hair.

"Enough," he murmured, and she relaxed her hands. "Sheathe your claws, woman."

Smiling, she sucked his sated cock, loving the feel of him relaxing against her tongue. Eliciting a deep sigh, he gazed down at her while he stroked her jaw.

"*Siora...*" he whispered, the word reverent upon his lips.

Releasing him from her mouth, she smoothed her hands over his thighs. "You look like you're about to collapse."

His lips formed a sexy, sated smile before he lowered to the mat, drawing her into his arms before collapsing on his back. Siora shimmied into his side and rested her chin on her fist as her elbow pushed into the mat.

"I like making you feel good," she said, trailing her finger over his cheek.

Encircling her wrist, he lifted her hand to his lips and kissed her palm. "Sweetheart, if you only knew. I swear, I'm going to make you feel good too. I just need to catch my breath."

She made a *tsk, tsk, tsk* sound. "That's unacceptable, General. You need to be in tip-top shape for our upcoming battle."

Laughing, he arched a brow. "Is that supposed to be an impression of me telling you to perform better on the field?"

Closing an eye, she glanced at the ceiling. "Maaaaaaybe."

"Okay, I'm a tyrant. I get it," he teased.

"You're not, but it was fun to hate you just a little."

His lips formed an adorable pout, sending her heart into overdrive. "You don't still hate me, do you?"

"Debatable," was her cheeky reply.

Breathing a laugh, he shook his head against the mat. "No way. You couldn't destroy me like you just did if you detested me. No one is *that* good of an actress."

She mimicked flicking her hair over her shoulder. "Maybe I missed my calling."

"Okay, Meryl Streep. Let's leave the acting to the humans."

Grinning, she relaxed into him as they softly stroked each other. Finally, he broke the silence, a slight hesitancy in his tone.

"It's up to you if you still want to spar in the evenings. You've corrected the tell with your hip, but I'm happy to keep training you. I think it's helping to improve your overall performance on the field."

Contemplating, she traced a finger over the scratchy hairs on his chest. "Are you saying that because you want to keep fucking me?"

Sliding his fingers under her chin, he gently lifted it to claim her gaze. "Yes. I don't want to lie to you. I love the time we spend together training *and* fucking. I don't think there's anything wrong with that."

"It would hurt my career if anyone finds out," she said, fangs toying with her lower lip as she searched for the words. "We have to keep it secret until it ends."

An unreadable reaction flickered in his eyes. "If that's what you want."

Feeling her eyes dart between his, she asked, "Isn't that what you want? Once the conflict with Bakari is over, there will be no need for me to train this vigorously for combat."

"We'll both still be in the army, Siora. I'll still see you unless you're dead set on avoiding me."

She wrinkled her nose. "I know. But you'll be back at Valeria and will resume your life there. I'll hopefully become head of security at Lynia, but I'll still just be Luthor's daughter from a meager farm on a rural compound."

"That's not how I see you," he said, running the backs of his fingers over her cheek.

"How do you see me?" she asked before she could stop the words from tumbling out of her mouth. Goddess, she sounded desperate and realized with each vibrant pound of her heart how important his answer was to her.

"As a beautiful, fierce warrior. One who will partner with me to protect our people in the battle against Bakari."

Her lips twitched. "I guess Latimus told you."

Nodding, he cupped her jaw. "I'm proud to have you as my first-in-command at the final battle. I can think of no one I'd rather have by my side."

Tears burned her eyes, making her feel vulnerable, and she willed them away. Sentiment and feelings had no place between them. They were teammates who gave each other pleasure, and she would do well to remember that before she did something completely stupid like fall in love with him.

"Well, I'll do my best to make sure you don't get bludgeoned," she teased, attempting to lighten the heavy mood. "And then, we'll both go on to build our lives on Valeria and Lynia. It will be nice to be free from war for once."

Deep brown eyes skated over her face as he studied her. "If that's what you want," he repeated, running his thumb over her lip.

Lifting a shoulder, she grinned. "I think it's just how it is. In the meantime, I'd like to continue training with you at night. I've learned a lot and definitely see an improvement. I mean, if you have time. I don't want to drain you."

"I'll always have time for you," he murmured, the tender words squeezing every ounce of breath from her lungs. "You know that, right, sweetheart?"

Swallowing thickly, she commanded her heart to slow the fuck down. "Thank you."

"In the meantime, there's something I need to take care of."

Lifting her brows, she shot him a questioning look.

He lurched, encircling her with his arms and flipping them over as she yelped. Looming over her, he smiled. "You took my cock like a champ, honey. Now, I need to suck you dry. You ready?" Waggling his brows, he began to trail wet kisses down her neck, between the valley of her breasts, and over the quivering skin of her abdomen. Pressing his hands to her inner thighs, he gently spread them apart.

"Are they your favorite?" he asked, running his hands over the soft fabric of her yoga capris.

"My yoga pants? Not really."

"Good." Gripping the hem, he ripped the pants in half, destroying the garment before tossing it aside.

"I really like this whole 'ripping my clothes' thing you've got going on," she said, smiling down at him as she made quotation marks with her fingers. "Not great for my workout attire, but *really* sexy, General."

His lips curved into a sexy grin as he palmed her thighs and pushed them wide. "If I have it my way, I'll rip every damn piece of clothing you own." Blowing on her drenched core, his eyes swam with amused desire. "Now, be a good little vixen and let me taste you, honey."

He dove into her pussy, causing her back to arch as she thrust her fingers in his thick hair. And then, she closed her eyes and let him return the very pleasurable favor.

Chapter Nine

A week later, Garridan stood in front of the mirror straightening the bow tie that went with his tuxedo. He hadn't dressed up in ages and could barely remember how to tie the damn thing. Deciding it looked fine, he gave a sigh and leaned down to grab his tuxedo jacket. Sliding it on, he assessed his reflection.

He looked like the aristocrat his father had always wanted him to be, and something about that rankled the hell out of him. If he weren't escorting Celine, he would've just worn a suit and called it a day. But tongues wagged throughout aristocratic circles at Valeria, and he didn't want to hurt her reputation. She was still looking for a bonded mate, and he wanted to look his best to support her.

Once he was fully dressed, he headed out, locking the door behind him and trailing down the front porch stairs. Glancing at his parents' mansion, he noted the windows were dark and assumed they were already at Valeria's main castle.

His shoes clacked against the pavement as he took the fifteen-minute walk to Celine's home. It was a nice evening, and he figured it was best spent in the fresh air rather than driving a four-wheeler. In truth, he would've much rather spent it with Siora, training her before they fell into one of their earth-shattering love-making sessions. But the army needed his father's donation, and he would escort Celine to ensure it happened.

It was the first night he hadn't spent with Siora since they began their sessions almost two weeks ago. Although it was a short time, it somehow felt like an eternity. Not in a bad way, he thought, grinning. Goddess, no. In the best way, like the fairy tales that spoke of the eternity of peace and goodness that existed in Etherya's realm before the War of the Species.

Like the kind of eternity you wanted to continue...long as you both shall live...

The inner thoughts were serious and ones Garridan had never had about another. Sure, he'd courted women off and on over the centuries, but none had even come close to taking up residency in his brain like Siora. At this point, her face was emblazoned in his mind, and he'd even begun to dream of her at night.

"You're getting sentimental in your old age, soldier," he muttered, inwardly chuckling at his sappiness.

But the truth was, he had lived for ten centuries, blazing a path as a competent soldier and advisor to Commander Latimus. When the War of the Species ended two decades ago, they had a brief moment of peace in which Garridan considered settling down...before Bakari appeared and upended that notion. Now, if they vanquished Bakari, he would finally have an opening to consider settling down and having children.

He'd always thought of having kids one day, but it seemed a faraway dream—one he would consider when he met someone compatible enough to understand his desire to protect the kingdom would always rank highly as he built his family. Siora sometimes uttered her belief he would bond with an aristocrat one day, but Garridan didn't see that making him happy. Aristocratic women wanted patrician bonded mates who held prominent positions in their kingdom, not soldiers who worked tirelessly and didn't give a damn about rank or privilege.

If he were honest, he could see himself settling down with Siora. She was a bit rough around the edges, but damn, that was one of the things he admired most about her. She was honest and straightforward, and it was so refreshing after being raised in a stuffy society where people only spoke their minds in dark corners behind others' backs.

And there was one other thing: Siora was achingly beautiful and hands-down the best lover he'd ever had. If he could stare at her stunning face and hold her until the world turned to dust, it wouldn't be long enough. She sometimes spoke of how she wasn't pretty and her body wasn't womanly, and he longed to reassure her. To him, she was the essence of beauty. Much more so than someone like Celine, who seemed more like a porcelain doll than the real, visceral woman Siora was.

Unfortunately, Siora had made it quite clear she didn't see a future between them. He couldn't tell if it was because she didn't want to settle down, didn't want to share a future with him, or truly just saw their trysts as a fun outlet to let off steam. Every time he had the urge to tell her he would consider trying to make their arrangement more serious, she shut him down. Not in a mean way. No—it was more...resigned, if anything. As if she simply couldn't contemplate them having anything more than the scant moments they stole after their training.

It frustrated Garridan, but he didn't want to push her, knowing her well enough to understand that would make her close up even more. She responded to his stern urgings on the field, but on a personal level, she didn't receive them the same way. Since he longed for her to be open with him, he usually conceded, allowing her to steer the direction of their conversations...allowing her to assert they didn't have a place in each other's lives.

"Well, hello. Is this my handsome date?"

Celine's wispy voice dragged him from the depressing thought as he trailed down the sidewalk to her house.

"It is indeed," he said, offering his arm. She wore the long, red gown of a Vampyre aristocrat and looked stunning as she slid her arm into his.

"I hope I don't fall. I'm wearing new heels, and I already want to burn them."

Laughing, he escorted her down the walkway and onto the sidewalk so they could stroll to the castle. "You look lovely, Celine. Are you trying to impress anyone in particular?"

Red splotches appeared on her cheeks as she grinned. "I fear you know my secret, so let's just get it out in the open. I'm hoping Sebastian asks me to dance even though he's bringing Mila."

"Since we're being honest, why don't I help? I can be your wingman."

"And dupe your own brother?" She arched a straw-colored brow. "How scandalous."

"Valeria could use a good scandal. We haven't had one in a while. And I think it's time my brother stopped focusing so much on his council seat and actually spent time outside of his duties. You two would make a nice couple, Celine."

"He doesn't even know I exist," she murmured, clutching his arm. "And I'm not...well, I'm not... Oh, this is so embarrassing..."

"You're not experienced?" Garridan asked in a supportive tone. "There's nothing wrong with that. I have it on good authority my brother hasn't been with anyone in a long time. Let's knock his socks off tonight. I'll dance with you, and we'll try to get him to notice you in that gorgeous dress. If he can stop talking to Governor Camron about the upcoming infrastructure project for more than two seconds, I think he'll fall under your spell."

"You have much more confidence than I, General, but I will try."

Giving her a reassuring nod, he led her to the castle, ready to endure what was sure to be a boring but necessary evening.

Chapter Ten

Siora buckled her strappy flat sandal and straightened, brushing her hands over the smooth fabric that covered her thighs. Donning her favorite pair of silver earrings, she headed into the living room where her father sat by the fireplace.

"You look lovely, dear," Luthor said, eyes sparkling from the nearby embers. "You even did something to your hair."

"I sort of, um, spiked it with gel," she said, circling her hand over her head. "I don't know, I figured it would go with the theme. I refuse to wear a dress because I detest them, but I bought this jumpsuit from one of the Lynian street vendors a few years ago, and I don't hate it."

"It's perfect for you and still very formal." Standing, he approached and kissed her on the cheek. "It is an honor for you to attend the fundraiser as Commander Latimus's special guest. I couldn't be prouder."

"I can't believe he asked me," she said, still in shock from when Latimus approached her earlier that afternoon. "He wants to introduce me to Queen Miranda and Governor Evie. Says we're three of a kind. I mean, I'm going to meet the queen. Holy shit." She lifted her hands, eyes wide as she shook her head.

"And you deserve it. It was nice of Latimus to let you borrow the four-wheeler."

"It's the fastest way to get to Valeria." Trailing over to the table by the front door, she began packing a small purse. "The compounds have been relatively safe from attacks lately, but I'll have this baby on me." Lifting her Glock, she ensured the safety was on and stuck it in her bag. "Can't be too prepared."

"Or too careful," he said, walking her to the door. "I'll be asleep when you get home, but I can't wait to hear about it tomorrow night when we have dinner."

"Thanks, Dad. Lock both deadbolts behind me, okay?"

"Stop worrying about your old man," he said, shooing her out the door. "I've survived this long, haven't I?"

Chuckling, she gave him one last peck and trailed to the four-wheeler. Once inside, she was thankful for the gob of gel she put in her hair. She usually didn't bother since she kept it short, but it would maintain the style so she looked presentable to all the fancy people who would be at the fundraiser. Of course, that included Garridan, which made her heart tumble in all sorts of directions.

He'd informed her he was attending tonight and had promised to resume their training the following evening. Would he be surprised when she showed up? Latimus's invitation was last-minute, and she didn't think Garridan knew she was attending. Would he ask her to dance, or would he rather keep up the pretense of them just being comrades? Perhaps he wouldn't want to dance with a poor farmer's daughter in front of the plethora of aristocrats who would be in attendance.

He often spoke of how he'd left the aristocratic life behind, but that was easy to say when you weren't surrounded by a roomful of peers. Narrowing her eyes, she contemplated as she drove through the grassy fields that separated Lynia and Valeria. Regardless, she wished to keep their relationship secret as well, and there was really no point in pondering things that were pointless.

Forty-five minutes later, she pulled up to Valeria's main gate. After stating her name, which Latimus had put on the list, the guards ushered her inside, and she drove toward the governor's castle that sat in the middle of the compound. The mansion was brightly lit, and she could hear music wafting from the ballroom inside. Parking her vehicle, she slung her purse over her shoulder and headed inside.

Nerves tingled within as she grabbed one of the champagne flutes from a server who passed by with a tray. Taking a large gulp, she reminded herself that she was the guest of Commander Latimus, the esteemed brother of King Sathan. Siora had always possessed an inner self-confidence, and she clutched onto it as she searched the room.

"Siora!" Latimus called, grinning as he trailed toward her. He looked handsome in a tuxedo with his slicked back hair and ice-blue eyes. A stunning blond woman accompanied him, and Siora knew it was his bonded mate, Lila.

"You must be Siora," she said with a tilt of her head. "I'm so honored to meet you. Latimus and Jack speak so highly of you."

"Thank you…" She trailed off, not knowing how to address the woman who was a respected diplomat in their kingdom.

"Just Lila is fine," she said, grinning. "Although I was born a stuffy aristocrat, my bonded mate is trying to break me of my formality. I think he's done a pretty good job so far."

"You still made me wear this monkey suit," Latimus muttered, sticking his finger in between his collar and neck and tugging. "I hate these things."

"You look very handsome," she said, tone stern as she smoothed his jacket. "If your son and Garridan can tolerate the tuxedo, you can too."

"Jack wore a tuxedo to make you happy, and so did I. You'll owe me later," he murmured, giving her a sultry look.

Lila's cheeks turned seven shades of red as she swatted his arm. "Latimus! We're in public. Please excuse my bonded's rudeness."

He scrunched his features at her as Siora held back a chuckle.

"Anyway, I'm so thrilled to meet the first woman battalion leader. How exciting. I can't wield a weapon to save my life."

"She just wields my balls instead—"

"Hush," Lila scolded, glancing around the room. "Camron will have a fit."

"Governor Camron can suck it, but I'll let it go," he said when she opened her mouth to argue. "Let me call over Miranda and Evie," Latimus said, turning and waving to them. They trailed over as Siora's heart leaped into her throat.

"We finally meet the magnificent Siora," Queen Miranda said, grinning from ear to ear beneath her olive green eyes and black, shoulder-length hair. "I'm honored."

"It is me who is honored to meet you, Queen Miranda," she said, dropping into a curtsy she hoped didn't look idiotic. "And you as well, Governor Evie. Thank you so much for having me."

The half-sisters gave each other a look before grimacing.

"Good lord, Siora, please don't bow to me. I hate all this formal crap. Why didn't you tell her I hate the formal crap?" Miranda asked Latimus, slapping him on the arm.

"Hey!" he said, swatting away her hand. "My wife has already landed a blow there, Miranda. Ease up."

"I tried like hell to get this caveman to let women into the army for years," Evie said, pointing to Latimus with her thumb. Her green eyes mirrored Miranda's, although she had fire-red hair atop her stunning face. "Thank you for proving me right."

"About what?" Siora asked, eyebrows lifting.

"That we're just as capable as men. More so, if you ask me. Welcome to the kick-ass females club, honey. Dear ol' sis and I saved you a seat," she said, jerking her head toward Miranda. "It's a super-fun club, and we're glad to have you."

Miranda and Evie were both fierce warriors who'd fought in battles decades ago, before women could formally join the army. They were legends in Siora's mind, and Evie's words spurred intense pride deep within.

"Thank you, Governor Evie and Queen Miranda. I'm so honored to fight in our army and protect our people."

"Just Miranda is fine," she said with a nod. "Thank you for coming tonight, by the way. I'd like to introduce you to some of the aristocrats if you don't mind. There are some rich widows I think support females in the army even if they're silent about it. I think you'll help me garner some extra donations. These wars are expensive, and we need the aristocrats' money to fund them. Believe me, we all pretty much detest the formality, but it's a necessary evil."

"Parade me to whomever you like," Siora said, smiling as she lifted her arms. "I'm happy to help the cause."

"Good. Let me grab some booze before we start the rounds," Miranda said, giving a playful grimace. "Need to dull the senses before I start to schmooze aristocrats."

"Me too," Evie said. "Nice to meet you, Siora."

After they left in search of a drink, Lila asked Latimus to dance, causing the commander to give an annoyed eye roll. Still, he led his bonded mate onto the floor, showcasing how much he loved her even though Siora could tell he'd rather be stabbed by a thousand Deamons than dance.

Sipping her champagne, Siora studied the room, refusing to admit she was searching for Garridan. Finally, she saw his broad shoulders where he stood across the large ballroom next to a willowy, golden-haired woman. *Celine*. Bristling, Siora watched as he slid his arm around Celine's shoulders, tugging her to his side. Smiling down at her, he whispered something in her ear before she tilted her head back and laughed.

The pale line of her throat glistened in the light of the chandelier beneath her perfect fangs, and Siora felt tears sting her eyes. Goddess, she was so pretty. Draped in her formal gown with long, flowing fabric, she looked like a statue of a beautiful goddess. Glancing down at her black jumpsuit and flat sandals, Siora realized how stupid she must look. She would never be in the same league as Celine when it came to appearance.

A small kernel of anger began to well in her gut, growing to a ball of full-on fury as she observed them together. He'd had ample time to tell her he was escorting Celine to the fundraiser. Hell, he'd been *inside* her every night for two fucking weeks. But he hadn't thought to mention it. He hadn't even thought to ask her if *she* might want to accompany him.

"Why would he?" Siora muttered to herself. "What aristocrat would ask a farmer's daughter to a fundraiser? Stop being ridiculous, Siora."

It was irrefutable proof she was right about their circumstances. Two people as different as she and Garridan would never be able to forge a life together. She would never fit into his world of wealth and privilege, and he certainly wouldn't be happy as the bonded mate of a female warrior on a rural compound.

And still...even though she knew it was futile, Siora longed for it anyway. Goddammit, she'd begun to yearn for things that were all but impossible.

Annoyed at herself and angry at him for not telling her he was bringing Celine, she clenched the glass. Reminding herself not to shatter the damn thing, she chugged the rest of the contents and set it on one of the trays that lined the wall.

Why in the hell hadn't he told her? She wouldn't have been upset he was bringing a date—that was standard at these events—but the fact he omitted the information, especially since they'd been spending so much time together, pissed her off. And, honestly, it just fucking hurt. After all the times they'd been intimate...and he'd stared deep into her eyes as he claimed her...didn't that matter enough for him to tell her he was choosing to bring someone else to a public event?

"You told him you didn't want anything serious, Siora. No labels. He's just following your directive."

As she stood in the corner murmuring to herself like a dolt, she realized she wished he hadn't listened to her. That he'd tossed her insistence aside and reassured her they could make it work somehow. *Stupid fucking daydreams.* She was really getting aggravated at the asinine musings that became more imprinted in her mind every damn day. Sighing, she straightened as Miranda approached from the corner of the room.

"Okay, I'm pleasantly buzzed and ready to dazzle some old rich dudes," Miranda said, eyes slightly glazed. "You with me? We're in this together now."

Brushing away her doubts, Siora nodded, ready to help her queen. She would deal with Garridan another time, when her heart didn't feel like a jumbled mess of scattered glass inside her chest.

Chapter Eleven

G arridan spotted Siora out of the corner of his eye, surprised she was at the event. Wondering why, he approached Latimus as he exited the dance floor with Lila.

"You invited Siora?"

"It was last-minute," Latimus said, nodding. "Miranda thought she could help raise some money as one of our preeminent female soldiers. And I think she just wanted to meet her."

"Right," Garridan said, rubbing the back of his neck. "Makes sense."

Latimus's eyes narrowed. "Should I have...told you? I know you've become friendly during the training, but I also didn't think it was a big deal."

"I..." He worked his jaw, realizing he should've told Siora he was escorting Celine. "No, it's fine."

"Look, Garridan," he said, placing his hand on his shoulder, "I don't want to get involved in your personal business. All I care about is that you two will be able to lead the battalions against Bakari. Is this going to jeopardize that somehow?"

"You know me better than that, Latimus," he said as annoyance flared. "I just wish I'd known, but it's no big deal."

"Sorry, brother. I didn't mean to make things awkward."

"It's fine. By the way, nice job on the dance floor."

Grimacing, Latimus ran a hand over his face. "If I didn't love my bonded so much, I'd never set foot near a dance floor. The things we do for our women. She's turned me into a fucking sap."

"It looks good on you, man. May we all be so lucky to find our one true mate."

"Truer words." Craning his neck, he gave a short nod. "Speaking of, she's summoning me. Let me know if you need me to smooth anything out with Siora."

Garridan nodded before Latimus walked away, and he glanced toward Siora. Miranda was leading her around the room, introducing her to various aristocrats as she reaffirmed they needed donations to fight the war against Bakari. He was viscerally aware of Siora, as he always was, and knew she felt his gaze. The muscle in her jaw clenched several times, and he understood she was pissed, which in turn spurred frustrated anger in his own gut.

He would've loved nothing more than to escort Siora as his date for all to see, but she'd been very clear their relationship was casual and she wished for it to remain secret. Compound that with the fact his father had bribed him into escorting Celine, and he was left with his current clusterfuck. Garridan hadn't mentioned he was bringing Celine because he didn't think it mattered. Damn it. Now, it looked as if he were hiding something, which wasn't true.

Sighing, he resumed his place at Celine's side, vowing to keep his promise to be her wingman. There would be time to deal with the situation with Siora later. For now, he had a vested interest in seeing his brother find happiness, and the more time he spent with Celine, he felt they would make a fantastic match. His brother was a self-proclaimed bachelor who spent way too much time on his aristocratic duties. Garridan knew life was short and wished for his brother to find a companion, someone who made him laugh and held him when he needed affection.

Someone who made him feel what Siora inspired every time Garridan was in her presence. By the goddess, he loved spending time with her and had no idea what he would do

when their one-on-one sessions ended. Thinking about it generated a feeling of intense
melancholy, so he just let it simmer as he re-
joined Celine.

The fundraiser dragged long into the night,
Siora avoiding him the entire time. She barely
made eye contact with him for the few minutes
they spoke when Miranda introduced her to
Celine and Sebastian. And finally, when he was
ready to walk Celine home, Garridan searched
the entire ballroom for Siora, realizing she'd
already left without saying goodbye.

S iora sat on Garridan's darkened porch,
thankful for the plushy outdoor chairs that
lined the expansive structure. She guessed the
home to be five or six bedrooms minimum.
Not as large as his parents' mansion, which
bordered his property, but still sizable. Aristocrats flaunted their wealth, and Astaroth had
his family's crest emblazoned atop the large
black gate that surrounded his property, which
meant Garridan's home was easy to find.

She'd debated confronting him tonight. After
all, she was angry, and that never led to a pro-
ductive discussion. But she felt it was best to
tell him she wished to end their sexual rela-

tionship. After tonight, there would be no more one-on-one training. They would fight together in the final battle, and she would build her life at Lynia. A life without the handsome soldier who'd become the focus of her every damn thought.

He walked into her line of view, his broad shoulders visible in the moonlight as he strode on the sidewalk. Unlocking the gate, he stepped through and closed it behind him. He didn't acknowledge her as his shoes clacked on the pavement of the walkway that led to the porch, but she knew he was aware of her presence.

Finally, he stopped before the porch steps and lifted his eyes to hers. "Hello, Siora."

"Hello," she said, lifting her brow. "Wasn't sure you'd be home tonight, but I figured I'd wait for a while before I went back to Lynia."

A muscle ticked in his jaw before he spoke. "Why'd you think I wouldn't be home?"

"I wasn't sure if you were fucking Celine," she said with a shrug. "Aristocratic women are taught to guard their virginity, but you never know. It always seemed like an antiquated rule to me."

His nostrils flared as anger clouded his expression. "Not to be a dick, but it's none of your business whether I'm fucking Celine or not."

Scoffing, she stood and ran her fingers through her hair. "Well, you've certainly made that clear—"

"No!" he interrupted, ascending the first step and jabbing his finger at her. "You do *not* get to pin this on me."

"Pin what on you?"

"The fact I escorted Celine to the fundraiser tonight. Not that you deserve an explanation, but my father blackmailed me into taking her. Otherwise, he was going to withdraw his donation for the new TECs."

Pursing her lips, she contemplated the words, wondering if they were true. "Well, you didn't seem like you were suffering, so I'm sure it wasn't a chore."

"There are things you don't know, Siora," he said, climbing another step. "Things I haven't told you because you insisted you wanted to keep this casual."

"Of course I want to keep it casual," she said, crossing her arms. "We have nothing but sex between us, and a romantic relationship would never work. Especially with our circumstances."

Cresting the last step, he towered over her as he gazed into her eyes. "Circumstances are what you make of them. I think it's time we started truly communicating, Siora." Glancing toward his father's home, he scowled. "My father will be home any minute, and I don't want him involved in this."

"Embarrassed he might see you with a poor farmer's daughter?" she asked, tapping her foot.

His eyes narrowed into angry slits. "You're really pissing me off right now. You came here looking for a fight, so let's have one. I think we should have it in private, in a language we'll both understand."

It sounded like a challenge, and she was intrigued. "Meaning?"

Stepping forward, he unlocked the door and gestured inside. "Come on."

She contemplated for several seconds before acknowledging his words held merit. In truth, she *was* looking for a fight and would rather have it without prying eyes so she could figure out why he didn't tell her about escorting Celine. Giving him a glare, she stepped inside before he closed the door.

Locking it, he began walking down the darkened hallway. "Follow me."

She complied, realizing she trusted him although she was mad as hell.

He led her through the home until they arrived at a back room. He flipped the switch, flooding the room with light, and she noticed the workout room filled with tons of weights, exercise machines, and a large black mat in the corner.

"You want a fight, so we'll have a fight," he said, stepping into the room and kicking off his dress shoes and socks. He tugged at his bow tie, pulling it off before he removed his jacket. After ditching the cummerbund, he began unbuttoning his shirt.

"Whoa," she said, stepping forward and holding up her hands. "What are you doing?"

"I'm getting ready to spar with you," he said, shrugging his shirt off his shoulders and tossing it aside. "At least combat is a language you understand." Trailing to the black mat, he stood in the middle and beckoned to her. "Come on. Let's fight, sweetheart. Tell me everything you came here to say. I can take it."

"I can't fight in this jumpsuit," she said, glancing down at the material. "It's the only nice piece of clothing I have."

"Then take it off," he said, arching an eyebrow. "It will certainly give you an advantage since I can barely think when you bare your skin to me, Siora."

"You want me to fight naked?" she almost shrieked. "Garridan—"

"If you don't think you can do it, I'll take your concession."

Bastard. As if she'd ever concede in *any* battle. "Are you fucking serious?"

His lips twitched. "Take off your clothes and fight me, Siora."

Huffing, she unclasped the button behind her neck, and the twin tufts of fabric that had been covering her breasts fell to her waist. Lust blazed in Garridan's eyes as she shimmied out of the jumpsuit and kicked her sandals aside. She left her panties on and trailed over to where he'd thrown his shirt, shrugging it on and cinching a few of the buttons. It fell to her knees, and she padded over to stand before him on the mat.

"This is ridiculous—"

His hand jabbed at her face, and she maneuvered away, her body instinctively knowing what to do after all her training. Gritting her teeth, she punched back, frustrated when he blocked her jab, and she turned to land a kick in his side.

Garridan muttered an *"oomph"* when she landed the kick before scuttling past her and grabbing her arm. Twisting it behind her back, he sandwiched it between them as his front pressed against her back.

"For the last time," he breathed in her ear, "I'm not fucking Celine. I don't *want* Celine. There's only one woman I want."

Grunting, she twisted out of his grasp and kneed him in the stomach before he doubled over. Grasping his thick hair, she jerked his head to stare into his eyes. "You were all over her tonight."

Quick as lightning, he jolted away, rotating to slide his arms around her waist and lift her before slamming her onto the ground. He was careful, as he always was when they sparred, but it knocked the breath from her lungs.

"I think she'd be a good match for my brother. We came up with a stupid plan to make him see her in a more flattering light. Like I said, there are things you don't know, Siora."

Placing her hands flat beside her head, she kicked her feet high and used the momentum to jump into a wide-legged stance. "You should've told me you were going with her."

"Yes," he said, crouching and lifting his hands to protect his face from any future blows. "I'm sorry I didn't tell you. I didn't think you wanted to know personal details about my life. I don't know what the rules are here."

"There are no rules," she said, although the words didn't ring true. "We're just fucking."

Amber eyes darted between hers before he whispered, *"Liar."*

"Don't call me names," she gritted as confusing emotions welled within. "And it's time to end this, Garridan. No more training, and no more fucking. It's over."

His features softened as he gazed at her. "Is that what you really want?"

"It doesn't matter what I want!" she yelled. *"This* can never happen." She gestured back and forth between them.

"Why?" he asked, slowly approaching her, palms held high as he assessed her. "You've made up some story in your head that isn't true, Siora."

"Of course it's true," she said, mortified when a single tear slipped down her cheek. Swiping it away, she held out her hand. "Don't come any closer."

"I'm beginning to think you say things you don't mean, sweetheart," he said, continuing to slowly approach her. "I think you're dying for me to touch you."

Her chin trembled as she shook her head. "No, I'm not."

The corner of his lips curved, the smile both sexy and filled with compassion. "Man, you're a really bad liar."

Eliciting a ragged cry, she lurched forward, aiming a punch at his jaw while attempting to swipe his leg. He anticipated the move, grabbing her wrist before swiping her legs instead and sending them both crashing to the floor. Tangled together, they struggled as he held her down with his large body, half-sprawled over hers.

"Damn it," he grunted, struggling to catch her wrists, one in each hand. Lifting them above her head, he held them there as they panted. Warm breaths mingled as their gazes remained locked, both too stubborn to look away.

"Let me go," she said, hating the sound of her voice, so weak. So much like the simpering woman she never wished to be.

His throat bobbed before he slowly shook his head. "I can't," he whispered, staring into her with such raw affection she felt her body melt beneath him. "Haven't you realized I can't let you go?"

"You don't want someone like me," she whispered, shaking her head upon the mat. "I don't fit in your world. *We* don't fit."

Settling into the juncture of her thighs, he pressed his straining erection into her core, causing her to moan. "I think we fit just fine, Siora. In all the ways that count. You're the sexiest woman I've ever seen, and I love that you fight as well as you fuck. What else do we need?"

"I never wanted a mate," she warbled, his face slightly blurred by the wetness in her eyes. "I don't know how to do this. I'm..." She stopped before admitting she was scared. The words made her feel too vulnerable as he stared at her with such longing.

"I know," he whispered, lowering to nudge her nose with his. "I am too. I never wanted a mate either, but sometimes, life doesn't go as planned."

"It will never work," she whispered, pleading for him to understand they had no future.

Forming a slow grin, he shook his head. "Thank the goddess I've always been an optimist, because you've definitely got the gloom and doom part down."

A breathy laugh escaped her throat. "I just don't want to set us up for failure. There are so many reasons—"

"Siora?" he interrupted, releasing one of her wrists and covering her lips with his fingers. "Will you do me a favor?"

Feeling her eyes dart between his, she nodded.

"Shut the fuck up and kiss me."

Lowering his head, he consumed her lips, drawing her against him as she surged her tongue inside his mouth. He groaned, low and raw, into the back of her throat, causing her arousal to rush between her thighs. Craving him more than her next breath, she tugged at his pants as he viciously kissed her, pulling them off his legs before he ripped her panties off. With his lips still cemented to hers, he plunged into her body, causing her hips to buck as his shaft claimed every inch of her wet, throbbing core.

"Yesss…" he hissed, furiously pumping his thick, pulsing cock into her taut channel as she sucked his tongue for dear life. He speared it into her mouth, mimicking the frenzied juts of his shaft, and her eyes rolled back in her head as she gave into the delicious pounding.

"Just like that," he rasped, gripping her thigh and wrapping it around his waist. "I love it when you relax like that when I'm deep inside you, sweetheart. Do you know how good it feels to have you open up like this when I fuck you?"

She wanted to tell him it was terrifying. That opening herself up to anyone was terribly disconcerting for the strong woman she'd always had to be. One who blazed her own path and never needed anyone. Never needed a partner. Of course, it was impossible to tell him that when her body had all but disintegrated into a pile of inflamed arousal as he consumed her with his words and his touch.

"I'm not stupid enough to let you go, Siora." Clenching his fingers in her short hair, he tugged, forcing her eyes to fly open. "It's not happening, so stop making excuses for why it won't work. Do you hear me?"

Her mouth fell open as he hammered inside her trembling body, and she struggled to answer. The overwhelming sensations were just too damn much.

Sliding his hand between their bodies, he ran his fingers through her slick essence, which now coated her folds and inner thighs, lubricating them before finding her clit. Stimulating the engorged nub with his fingers, he pressed his forehead to hers as they reached for the peak.

"Oh, *god*, I'm going to come," she wailed, his fingers maddening on the nerve-filled bud of her clit. "I can't take it."

"You can take it," he murmured, lips vibrating against hers as their faces pressed together. "Open that pretty pussy and come all over my cock, Siora. *Now.*"

Tossing her head back, she succumbed to the pleasure, feeling her body snap as he continued to piston deep within. He was everywhere—inside her body...inside her brain...inside her *heart*. Something bloomed in the deep confines of her chest, and she understood that as her body was shooting over the precipice of pleasure, her heart was undeniably falling into the abyss for the magnificent Vampyre who was loving her so vehemently. Crying his name, she clutched her arms around his neck and buried her face in the juncture between his nape and shoulder.

The vein that ran from his neck to his heart pulsed against her cheek, and she longed to plunge her fangs into the tender flesh; to drink from him as bonded mates often drank from each other when they shared bouts of pleasure.

"One day, sweetheart," he rasped, reading her thoughts as if she'd sent them to him in fucking bold text. "One day, we'll drink from each other while we do this."

The words were serious, causing her to thrust her nails into his upper back. The action elicited a ragged moan from him before he snapped, freezing for a millisecond before plummeting into his own orgasm. Bucking above her, he shot his release into her body, spraying her with his essence so it mingled with her own. Every part of their bodies connected as she lay below him trying to make sense of the earth-shattering experience. Small, visceral grunts escaped his throat as he lunged into her...once...twice...and one last time before he elicited a soft, sexy wail. Gathering her against his body, he slid his arms under her back and held her close, pressing his face into her neck.

They lay there, sated and replete, silent as their labored breaths echoed against the walls. Eventually, their bodies cooled, and Siora melded into the mat, her eyelids heavy as the cadence of his breathing began to slow. Expelling a long breath, she closed her eyes, promising herself she'd only sleep for a moment.

An indiscernible amount of time later, she awoke to feel Garridan lifting her into his arms before trailing to the doorway of the gym. Flicking off the light, he carried her to his bedroom, sliding her between the sheets before crawling in behind. Drawing her close, he spooned her, resting his face against the back of her neck before falling into slumber.

She lay there terrified to clutch onto the happiness that wanted to envelop every cell of her frame. It was too overwhelming, and she panicked as his deep breaths warmed the sensitive skin of her neck.

After he lay still for several minutes, she quietly eased from his embrace and donned her clothes in the gym. Heading out the front door, she ensured the lock on the knob was secure and scurried back to the four-wheeler parked at the castle. Jumbled thoughts rushed through her brain during the short, brisk walk before she hopped into the vehicle and drove back to Lynia as fast as the damn thing would take her.

Chapter Twelve

G arridan awoke as the first light of dawn glowed outside his bedroom window. Rolling onto his back, he placed his hands under his head and stared at the ceiling. Siora had run away, and that was...well, he realized it was a natural progression in their complex relationship. It meant she was scared, and if he'd learned anything in his long life, it was that the greatest joy always resided on the other side of fear, *if* one was willing to take the leap.

Chewing on his inner lip, he contemplated the best path to take with Siora. After last night, there was no doubt he wanted to pursue her. Yes, the time for total honesty had arrived. Garridan had lived for ten centuries and never even come close to feeling about someone the way he felt about Siora. She was fierce and stubborn and so achingly beautiful. He didn't know if she wanted to build a family and understood they'd need to make their way to having that very serious discussion, but there were other things he needed to tackle first.

To begin with, he wanted to court her. Garridan saw the importance of spending time with her outside the army so she could get comfortable with him—and with the idea they were meant to be together. She swore they didn't belong in each other's world, but he saw that excuse for what it truly was: Siora wasn't sure he would choose her. Somewhere along the way, she'd decided an aristocrat didn't belong with a farmer's daughter, and the story had become her reality. Smiling, Garridan realized he couldn't wait to relieve her of that notion. The great thing about immortals? Well, they had a lot of time, and he was a very patient man. He would take time to court her as she deserved to be courted, until his stubborn mate rewrote the tragic story.

"You sound as sappy as Latimus, old man," he chided, running his hands over his face. "But damn, if she isn't your mate, then no one is."

The belief was embedded deep within, and he knew with a little time, Siora would see the light as well. In the meantime, he would let her pull back as she seemed determined to do. He'd give her some space and take the gamble she would eventually realize she wanted to build something with him too. Hopefully, she would recognize they were perfect for each other and overcome her fear. He'd waited centuries to find his mate. Waiting a few weeks longer surely wouldn't kill him, although he certainly would miss her soft, silken skin and passionate kisses...and the way she moaned his name when he was deep inside her sweet body.

Feeling himself harden, he emitted a groan before lowering his hand to his shaft to ease his burgeoning erection, anticipating the next time Siora's firm grip would replace his own.

The next few days were chaotic for Siora as the final battle drew near. The timeline was established, and they would fight Bakari in a matter of days. As if that wasn't enough to process, Garridan had reverted to treating her like one of the soldiers, which rankled her. Yes, she'd bolted after their passionate night together, but she didn't expect him to act as if it didn't matter. The morning after, when she'd shown up on the battlefield, his expression was polite and detached, which worried her more than any flares of anger she'd ever observed.

"I'm sorry I left without saying goodbye," she said as the morning sun shined on the training field. "I needed to get home and change before training today."

"It's fine," he responded, his deep baritone sending shivers across her skin. "We need to focus on training since the final battle is near. I think you're right about ending our one-on-one sessions. You fixed the tell, and your combat skills have improved."

Kicking the grass with her boot, she nodded, understanding this meant they would end their sexual trysts too. "Okay. Thanks for...everything." Goddess, she sounded so lame.

"You're welcome." His eyes looked like melted amber in the glinting sunlight, and she almost wanted to weep for what she was throwing away. Reminding herself he was never hers to begin with, she braced herself and threw all her energy into training.

Throughout the training sessions, she and Garridan worked together to ensure their three battalions would be ready. During the battle, they would flank the north side of the forest along the field as Commander Kenden's troops flanked the south side. Bakari would certainly have Deamon troops hidden in the thick forests, and they would do their best to prevent casualties. Although Vampyres had self-healing abilities, they were still vulnerable to poison-tipped weapons that prevented self-healing. Siora was determined to ensure they didn't lose one Vampyre or Slayer soldier and took that vow very seriously.

The afternoon before the battle, Siora approached Garridan as he slung his backpack over his shoulder. "Can I talk to you for a minute before you head back to Valeria?"

"Sure."

They walked toward the edge of the field, and Siora noted most of the soldiers had already headed home. It was imperative they rest before they gathered early the next morning.

"Our battalions look good, and they're following our orders implicitly. I was a bit worried some of the male soldiers wouldn't accept a female as first officer, but it hasn't been an issue."

"Because you're a natural leader, Siora," he said, cupping her shoulder. "And you've excelled at every challenge. We're extremely prepared, and I fully expect our troops to shine."

She'd missed his touch, and his broad hand upon her shoulder caused her heart to pound. "And if we win, we'll be free of war. Hopefully." She lifted her hand, crossing her fingers.

Smiling, he nodded. "I hope so."

"I..." Glancing around, she told herself not to blurt out something embarrassing, such as how much she missed him. "Training with you was a fantastic experience. I really appreciate you taking the time to teach me."

"Sure." His eyes traveled over her face before he tilted his head. "Well, I'll see you in the morning. We'll meet here two hours before sunrise and load the troops into the utility vehicles before heading to the battlefield." Pivoting, he began to trail away.

"Wait," she called, grabbing his arm.

He turned, gazing at her, although his expression was unreadable.

"We said so many things the last night together, but we...we also *didn't* say a lot. I just... Fuck, I'm terrible at this." She released her grip and crossed her arms over her chest. "I expected you to be pissed I left that morning."

Shaking his head, he lifted a shoulder. "We're past that, Siora."

Feeling her eyebrows draw together, she studied him. "Past what?"

"Past our petty arguments and base emotions. There's so much more beneath the surface. The question is, are we too afraid to dig deep and find it?"

Inhaling a deep breath, she pondered. "I don't know how to answer that."

Grinning, he gave a slight nod. "Let me know when you figure it out." With a small salute, he turned and meandered across the field. She still had the urge to call him back, but what could she say? *Leave your aristocratic life behind to bond with me?* The words sounded ridiculous as they clanked in her mind.

Lowering to the grass, she ran her hand over the soft blades as she contemplated. She'd always been so confident in her abilities as a soldier, and her determination and drive were unparalleled. But in her personal life? She'd never seen herself as anything outstanding. She'd always assumed she was a normal person destined to have one goal: to excel as a female in the army. But what if she allowed her confidence in her physical skills to extend to her personal life? To believe she deserved to marry an aristocratic man, love him with all her heart, and have him love her in return?

The sentiment seemed foreign to her, and she wrinkled her nose. When did she decide she wasn't good enough? It was so counterintuitive to her strength and inner fortitude. Lifting her face to the setting sun, she closed her eyes, allowing realization to wash over her.

"You've sold yourself short your whole life, Siora," she whispered. "You deserve success in your career and in *every* aspect of your life."

Smiling, she expelled a heavy breath, releasing her fears and doubts across the expansive field. Of course, they would continue to rear their head, but she had to embrace the belief she was worthy in *all* segments of her existence. Believing in herself as a warrior had always come naturally. Believing in herself as a person fully deserving of love and happiness was harder, but she was determined to release her fears.

Garridan's face flashed through her mind, increasing the longing she felt for him. Finally, she was ready to admit the truth: she cared for him and wanted to try to build something together. Hell, she was likely falling in love with him, which would be a first. It was daunting and a bit terrifying, but it also felt...*liberating*, as if she was emancipating those old, toxic beliefs and clutching onto something with so many exciting possibilities.

Would he accept her acknowledgment and want to court her? She had no idea, but judging by his words their last night together, he experienced some intense feelings for her too. Armed with that knowledge, Siora set her plan into motion. She would focus on the battle and ensure they prevailed. Once they defeated Bakari, she would approach Garridan and be completely honest about her feelings.

Excited for the future, she rose and wiped off the dirt before grabbing her bag and heading home. Siora had a battle to win, and she was ready to kick some ass.

Chapter Thirteen

The morning of the battle arrived, and Siora awoke with a fresh, vibrant energy. Embracing her feelings for Garridan had set something free deep inside, and she was ready to fight like hell so she could focus on the future.

Two hours before dawn, the Vampyre immortal battalions gathered. Latimus gave a rousing speech before they loaded into the armored vehicles and drove to the battlefield.

The combat would take place in an open field south of the Slayer compound, Restia. It was where the wall of ether stood that separated the human world from the immoral realm and therefore kept their people secret from humans. Etherya's world had existed this way for countless centuries, and the humans remained oblivious to their existence.

When they arrived at the battlefield, they prepared their battalions, and Siora and Garridan faced Latimus.

"May the goddess be with you," Latimus said, lifting his hand in a salute.

"May the goddess be with you, brother," Garridan said, saluting in return as Siora did the same.

Latimus and Garridan clenched each other's forearms, indicating their strong bond.

"We've fought so many battles together over the centuries," Garridan said. "Hopefully, this is the last one for a while."

"With Siora as your first-in-command, I have no doubt."

"Thank you, Commander Latimus," she said as nervous energy coursed through her body. "We'll stomp out every Deamon in the northern flank."

With one last nod, he returned to his own battalion while Siora and Garridan began to lead the troops. As they marched, Siora grinned at the strong, handsome general, acknowledging how happy she was to have him by her side.

"What's that smile for?" he murmured as the soldiers marched behind.

"I'll tell you afterward. Don't die, okay? I've got some really important shit I need to tell you."

His lips curved into that sexy smile she'd come to covet. "Can't wait."

They directed the troops across the north flank of the forest, preparing them for the imminent conflict. Bakari appeared, his throng of Deamon warriors close behind, and Siora double-checked the TECs lined on her weaponry belt. They were special weapons that would obliterate the immortal Deamons instantly, and she was ready to use every last one if needed.

Several loud cries sounded from the battlefield, and Siora drew her rifle around her shoulder, ready to defend her kingdom.

Multitudes of Deamon soldiers began to rush in from both sides—half from the main battlefield, and half from the nearby forest. She and Garridan commanded their soldiers to commence combat, and they were thrust into physical battle. Gritting her teeth, she got to work.

For long minutes, she attacked the barrage of soldiers, using her semi-automatic rifle as well as the TECs to eliminate them one by one. Garridan fought off to her side, and she caught glimpses of him from the corner of her eye, besting the Deamons as he'd done for centuries. An enemy soldier approached, knocking her rifle from her hand and sending it flying behind her back. Grasping one of the TECs, she deployed it, disintegrating the creature, but another one closed in behind. Realizing the TEC was out of deployments, she tossed it to the ground and reached for another.

The Deamon knocked her hand away, and she lunged forward, landing a punch in his throat, causing him to clutch it and gasp for breath. Reaching for her rifle, she tried to swing it around but felt a tug from behind. Another Deamon had grabbed the strap, and he pulled it from her body before turning it on her.

"Time to meet the goddess, Vampyre!" he spat, placing his finger over the trigger.

Instinctively reacting, she launched a laser-focused kick into his abdomen before he doubled over and dropped the rifle to the ground. Approaching, she began to fight the creature in one-on-one combat as he tried to fight back. Pride welled inside as she realized she was kicking his ass rather expertly, and a portion of her enhanced combat skill could be attributed to Garridan's training. Planting her weight on one leg—*without* dropping her hip—she launched into a jump kick and knocked the bastard to the ground. Grabbing a TEC from her belt, she plunged it into the Deamon's forehead and blew him to bits.

"Nice job not dropping your hip!" Garridan yelled from several feet away before he turned to fight an oncoming Deamon.

"Damn straight!"

They fought for what seemed like hours, although it was most likely minutes in the grand scheme of things. The immortal army was making slow, steady work of defeating the Deamons, and she remained focused as she fought.

A bright light exploded on the field, almost blinding her. Siora heard a gruff shout and saw Garridan clutching his lower neck before plunging a TEC into a Deamon's forehead and instantly killing him.

"Garridan!" she shouted, running toward him as she blinked away the brightness. Approaching his side, she saw him fall to the ground and crouched beside him.

"The bastard stabbed me with a poison-tipped sword, but I think I pulled it out quickly enough that my body will heal."

Examining the wound, she touched her fingers to it, softly pressing. "Yes, you just need some blood flow to the area. It's a surface wound. Thank the goddess."

Suddenly, her hand froze against his chest, and she struggled to move. Garridan froze too, and Siora gazed around the battlefield, realizing everything had come to a sudden halt.

"Callie has frozen everyone with her powers," came a voice over the walkie-talkie, and Siora recognized it as Nolan's, the kind Slayer physician who was stationed in the infirmary tent. "We're far away enough from the battlefield that it's not affecting our movements. Stay tuned for updates."

"I can't move anything below my neck," Siora said, willing her body to move. "I need to massage the area around your wound to increase blood flow. That will help counteract the poison. Shit!"

"It's okay," Garridan said, slightly rasping. "This most likely has something to do with the prophecy. I'm not dead yet."

"Don't joke about that," she said, emotion welling in her throat. "I mean it, Garridan. I have a lot of stuff to say to you, and I can't do it if you're dead."

Labored breaths exited his lungs as his fangs flashed in a smile. "I have a lot to say to you too. I was waiting for you to realize you can't live without me."

Breathing a laugh, she ached to hold him. "So, you were intentionally avoiding me."

"You needed space to figure things out. I understand you, Siora. You'll get that one day."

Their conversation was interrupted by several more bright flashes from the battlefield. All at once, every Deamon soldier who stood frozen on the battlefield disintegrated, each of them turning to dust and scattering over the field as if they'd never existed. A loud boom echoed across the field before Siora regained her ability to move.

Leaning over Garridan, she examined the wound that sat at the juncture of his neck and shoulder. "Here," she said, massaging it with her fingers. "We need to urge your blood to circulate around it so it expels the poison and you can heal." She maneuvered her fingers for a minute before he sat up and pushed the skin with his fingers.

"I think I'm good. That was a close one, but thankfully, Deamons have terrible aim."

Overcome with joy, she nodded. "They pretty much sucked. Did we win? What the hell happened?"

Lifting the small walkie-talkie from his belt, Garridan radioed Latimus. "Commander, the Deamons we were fighting seem to have disappeared. Am I imagining things?"

Latimus's voice crackled over the device. "Callie fulfilled the prophecy and defeated Bakari. In the meantime, she also somehow managed to destroy every soldier in his Deamon army and obliterate the ether."

Garridan's eyes grew wide as he looked at Siora. "So...we no longer have a barrier that shields us from the humans?"

"Looks that way. I'll know more when we debrief. In the meantime, I want to gather all our troops on the field and assess the damage and casualties, especially from our Slayer soldiers.

After that, we'll address them and send them home for a nice long break."

"Ten-four, commander. Siora and I will round everyone up and meet you at the center of the battlefield."

Placing the device back on his belt, he dug his hand into the ground to anchor himself to stand. Siora rose, extending her hand and helping him up.

"Thanks," he said, affection glowing in his deep brown eyes.

Giving a nod, she squeezed his hand before turning to face the soldiers. There would be time for them to say what needed to be said, but first, they had a job to do. Placing her fingers between her lips, she gave a loud whistle and circled her hand in the air.

"All battalions, assemble for roll call."

The troops began to gather in front of her so they could assess the formation before marching back to the main field.

Looking up at Garridan, she asked, "Do you want to do roll call?"

"No, ma'am. It's all you, Battalion Leader Siora. Go for it."

Grinning from ear to ear, she turned to face her battalions and commence her duties as a full-fledged officer in the immortal army.

Chapter Fourteen

After addressing the troops, Latimus informed them they would have a few weeks off to spend with their families and rest. Now that Bakari had been vanquished, his threat was diminished, but the destruction of the ether created a new set of challenges. Humans were wily creatures, armed with nuclear weapons and almost limitless technology, so the army would need to be refashioned into a force that could defend the immortals from an attack. Although Queen Miranda and King Sathan were working on a plan to approach the humans, only time would tell if they were friend or foe.

Siora headed back to the compound of Takelia in the armored vehicles and divested her weapons and combat gear before preparing to head home. Garridan approached her, a glint in his eye as he gave her that sexy grin.

"Heading home to the farm?"

"Yep," she said, placing her hands in her pockets. She desperately wanted to have some alone time with him but knew they were both exhausted.

"You know," he said, rubbing his chin, "after I go home and take a massive nap, I'd really like to head over to Lynia and see you. And maybe meet your dad."

Biting her lip to contain her grin, she shrugged. "I only introduce him to people who are really important to me."

Lifting his brows, his grin deepened. "Is that so?"

Nodding, she felt herself beaming like a lovesick dolt. As her heart pounded in her chest, she said softly, "You could come over for dinner. We're having Slayer blood and corn chowder. Dad loves food, even though we don't need it, and it's pretty much a staple at this point. Oh, and there will be wine too."

Affection swam in his eyes. "I'd love to come over for dinner."

"Sweet." Kicking the ground with the toe of her boot, she glanced around. "Don't tell anyone yet, okay? I want to talk to you first and figure out how we're going to do this. I don't want the soldiers thinking I got ahead from sleeping with my commanding officer."

"No one in their right mind would think that, but I understand." Glancing at his watch, he said, "I'll come over at six if that works."

"Perfect. See you then."

He gave her an almost imperceptible wink, visible only to her, that set her heart aflutter. Flashing one last grin, she hopped into a four-wheeler and drove home, anticipating her father's reaction when she informed him they were having company from a very handsome, eligible Vampyre. Knowing he'd be thrilled, she gave a tiny squeal—which was completely out of character for her, but so was falling in love, so she figured she'd just go with it.

As the wind whipped her hair, Siora took a moment to thank the goddess for their victory and for Garridan, the man who, somehow, had tunneled his way into her heart.

G arridan awoke from his nap rested and filled with anticipation about meeting Siora's father. It was a big step for them, and he understood how meaningful it was for her. Donning his black pants, polo shirt, and loafers, he marveled at how nice it felt to dress in something besides tactical gear for once. Locking the door behind him, he hopped into his four-wheeler and drove to Lynia.

The farm sat on the outskirts of the rural compound, and Garridan noticed the rows of corn that lined the field behind the small home. Now that Slayers and reformed Deamons lived on all the compounds, growing food was a lucrative business for Vampyres, who only needed Slayer blood for sustenance. Although Vampyres ate food for taste and pleasure, they didn't need it like other immortals.

Garridan climbed the front porch steps and lifted his hand to knock, but the door was swung open by a smiling Siora.

"You're right on time."

She looked beautiful in her casual attire, and her hair was fuller, causing him to wonder if she'd put something in it to style it.

"You look pretty."

Red splotches appeared on her cheeks, and she gestured him inside. "Thanks. We're almost ready. It's not as big as your house, but it does the job."

Garridan observed the dining room table lined with wine, corn, and goblets of Slayer blood before a man approached him, arms outstretched.

"General Garridan," he said, pulling him into a firm embrace. "It's so nice to meet you. I've heard wonderful things. Thank you for taking the time to train my Siora, and thank you for defending our people."

"You're welcome," he said, drawing back. "Siora is a talented soldier, and I'm glad Bakari's threat is quelled so we can hopefully enjoy some peace."

"Dad, you're smothering him," Siora said, tugging his arm. "Come on—let's eat. I'm starving."

They had a lovely dinner, filled with laughter and embarrassing stories from Siora's childhood that had her playfully rolling her eyes on more than one occasion. Garridan found Luthor a jovial man, and he was honored to be included in their small family gathering.

After dinner, Luthor retired to his room, and Garridan and Siora headed outside to sit on the couch that lined the far side of the porch. When he slid his arm around her shoulders, she nestled into his side, and he kissed her temple as they stared across the rapidly dimming horizon.

"Dad really likes you," she said, snuggling into him. "I can tell."

"I'm glad to hear it since I plan to see him quite often."

Pulling back, she tilted her head as her eyes glowed in the light of the newly risen moon. "You do?"

"Yes," he said, running the backs of his fingers along her jaw. "If that's all right with you."

Swallowing, she licked her lips, the gesture sending shards of desire through his veins. "There's so much to figure out if we really do this. I'm woman enough to admit I'm scared, but I also don't want to lose you. So I guess we need to figure some shit out."

Chuckling, he nodded. "For starters, I was thinking I might sell my house at Valeria. I have nothing tethering me there, and I can live on Lynia as easily as I can live there."

"But you haven't gotten your assignment yet," she said, eyebrows drawing together. "Latimus will certainly assign you to a high-ranking position. You'll most likely have to visit the military centers on each compound. Lynia is a distant compound and living here will require a ton of travel."

"Yes, but *you're* at Lynia, and I assume you want to remain close to your father. Plus, I'm sure Latimus will assign you as head of security for the compound."

Her eyes darted between his. "It's not fair of me to ask you to sell your home and move here."

"You're not asking. I'm offering of my own free will. I have no ties to Valeria since I'm not close with my parents, and I can continue to see Sebastian when I visit."

"Will you be happy on a rural compound? It's probably boring here compared to Valeria."

"If I'm with you, I'm pretty sure I'll be happy." Running his thumb over her cheek, his tone was reverent. "I want to court you, Siora, and when we're ready, I want to bond with you and build a future. If you want to have kids, we can work our way up to that too."

Her fangs toyed with her lip as she grinned. "I can see myself having kids down the road if I'm with the right person. It wasn't ever a pressing desire because I was so fixated on becoming a soldier, but it would be nice to build a family. And my dad would be thrilled to have some grandbabies. He would definitely offer to help so we could still build our military careers, which is pretty freaking awesome."

"I think we can build something amazing if we try, Siora. I've never wished for a bonded mate, but you burst into my life, and I fell for you before I even knew what was happening."

"I'm so honored you want to court me," she whispered, cupping his jaw. "You could have anyone, Garridan."

"I only want you, sweetheart. Don't you know that by now?" Pressing his lips to hers, he gave her a tender kiss before drawing back.

"Will your parents be upset you're settling with a commoner?"

"Probably," he said, arching an eyebrow. "But I just don't give a damn. It's my life, and I aim to live it exactly as I please."

"That's pretty badass for an aristocrat," she teased. "Who knew you guys had the ability to be tough?"

Lowering his hand, he tickled her side as she laughed before burying his face in her neck. Inhaling her fragrant scent, his body hardened as she shimmied into him.

"I want to drink from you," he whispered, nuzzling her neck. "Goddess, you smell so good."

Sliding her fingers into his hair, she gently tugged him closer. "Then drink from me."

Lifting his head, he gazed into her eyes. "That's a huge step, sweetheart. If I drink from you, I won't be able to let you go."

Clenching her fingers in his hair, she gave him a sultry smile as his cock jerked inside his pants. "I'm counting on it, General."

Emitting a low growl, he pressed his face to her nape, extending his tongue to lick the pulsing vein. His saliva would help prepare her sensitive skin for his invasion as well as numb the pain. Her body trembled beneath his as his tongue rasped over her skin, and he moaned before placing the tips of his fangs over her vein. Supporting her neck with his hand while the other one closed around her waist, he inhaled a sharp breath and pierced her sweet skin.

Her responding mewl sent shivers of lust through his frame as thick rivulets of blood coated his mouth. Drawing her between his lips, he drank her essence, imbibing everything that was his beautiful Siora. She whimpered beneath him, clutching his hair and shoulder as her fingernails dug into his scalp. Wracked with pleasure, he swallowed her sweet spirit until he felt himself begin to lose control. The scent of her arousal surrounded them, and if he wasn't careful, he'd rip her clothes off and fuck her right there on her father's front porch. Understanding that wasn't an option, he released her vein, resting his forehead against her as he licked the wound closed.

"Oh, god, I almost came," she whispered, the words ragged as she expelled heavy breaths. "I can't wait for you to do that when you fuck me."

"I can't wait either," he growled, placing a kiss on the spot, which was rapidly healing thanks to his saliva and her self-healing abilities. "And you're going to drink from me too."

"I'm so excited to taste the pure blood of a fancy aristocrat. Don't tell your father—he'll be scandalized."

Chuckling, he rested his lips against the shell of her ear. "Even more reason to spread the news far and wide."

Her laughter surrounded them as they cuddled together on the couch. As her fingers sifted through his hair, she whispered his name.

"Hmm?"

"I think...I think I'm in love with you."

Drawing back, he gazed into her stunning eyes. "That's good, because I think I'm in love with you too."

Her grin was adorable as she caressed his face.

"And if our kids grow up to have horrible tells when they fight, I'm blaming it on you."

"Hey!" she said, swatting him. "My tells were perfectly legitimate. I kicked your ass a time or two, didn't I?"

Chuckling, he drew her into a tender kiss. "You sure did. If we have kids, they're going to be tough as hell."

Wrapping her arms around his neck, her lips formed a beaming smile. "They'll be the best warriors in the kingdom. Can't fucking wait."

Consumed by her, Garridan trailed kisses over her face and neck before walking her inside and finishing the wine. Filled with the knowledge this would be the first night of so many spent together, he settled into his future with his magnificent Siora, the warrior who had stolen his heart and his perfect immortal mate.

Before You Go

T hanks so much for reading this fun, heart-felt, steamy story! I love when kick-ass women like Siora find their HEA. Hope you enjoyed it too! Thanks so much for spending some time in Etherya's Earth with me!

Have you read my **Prevent the Past** trilogy? It follows a brilliant scientist who must solve time travel and the handsome, mysterious soldier who offers his protection. *Let's just say LOTS of sparks fly!* Happy reading.

ALSO BY REBECCA HEFNER

Prevent the Past Series
Book 1: A Paradox of Fates
Book 2: A Destiny Reborn
Book 3: A Timeline Restored

The Etherya's Earth Series
Prequel: The Dawn of Peace
Book 1: The End of Hatred
Book 2: The Elusive Sun
Book 3: The Darkness Within
Book 4: The Reluctant Savior
Book 4.5: Immortal Beginnings
Book 5: The Impassioned Choice
Book 5.5: Two Souls United
Book 6: The Cryptic Prophecy
Book 6.5: Garridan's Mate
Book 7: Coming soon!

About the Author

USA Today bestselling author Rebecca Hefner grew up in Western NC and now calls the Hudson River of NYC home. In her youth, she would sneak into her mother's bedroom and read the romance novels stashed on the bookshelf, cementing her love of HEAs. A huge Buffy and Star Wars fan, she loves an epic fantasy and a surprise twist (Luke, he IS your father).

Before becoming an author, Rebecca had a successful twelve-year medical device sales career. After launching her own indie publishing company, she is now a full-time author who loves writing strong, complex characters who find their HEAs. Rebecca can usually be found making dorky and/or embarrassing posts on TikTok and Instagram. Please join her so you can laugh along with her!